Geoffrey Cush was born in Christchurch, New Zealand in 1956 and was educated at Nelson College with the sons of farmers and champion shearers. Afterwards he came to London where he drifted into the world of pornography, first as a bookshop assistant in Chinatown and later as a supervisor at the Nude Encounter parlour in Old Compton Street. He lost this job after allowing a reporter from the *News of the World* to become lodged in one of the booths, and thereafter pursued a career as a film-extra, maintaining his links with pornography by writing stories for *Vulcan* and other magazines. From there he progressed naturally to novel-writing.

Geoffrey Cush

GOD HELP THE QUEEN

First published in Great Britain in Abacus by
Sphere Books Ltd 1987
This paperback edition published in Abacus by
Sphere Books Ltd 1987
27 Wrights Lane, London W8 5TZ

Set in Trump

Printed and bound in Great Britain by
Cox & Wyman Ltd, Reading

To Peter Benedict

PROLOGUE

Christmas Day 1992
On television: Her Majesty The Queen

'In the New Year, we shall see a great change in our national life. The New Companies will bring a return to full employment. I am sure we all felt the excitement of queueing for our shares in them, of becoming our own employers. But we must also feel an increased sense of duty.

'Each field of industry will be co-ordinated under a central administration of top designers and marketing advisors. Divisive local competition will be curtailed, enabling us to concentrate on our foreign markets. The future success of Britain depends on the success of British products abroad. This means that each of us has vital work to do, and I would like now to talk about mine.

'My shares are in the Electronics New Company, which has developed the Britannia Box. This is a revolutionary product, a practical aid to the work and leisure of future generations. And you may ask how I could be of service to it, representing as I do everything that is old-fashioned, impractical and past. But I believe there is a way.

'When I come before you again, in a year from now, I

shall present the annual foreign sales figures for the Britannia Box. I know there will be pride in my voice then, the pride of real achievement. And I am certain that by next Christmas you will be able to say, "Yes, there is a place for monarchy in modern Britain. Yes, the Queen earns her keep, like everyone else."'

1

Michael Felter's deck chair was in the most upright position. He saw the attendant loping towards him across the park, and fished two fifty-pence pieces out of his pocket. He looked at them in the palm of his hand. One showed its date: 1979. The last Labour government had collapsed twenty-three years ago. The other coin showed helmeted Britannia.

He held them out to the attendant. 'Will it go up again next year?'

'I don't think so. It's quite a price now isn't it?'

He was a grinning Irish boy. One of the poorest. There were people worse off than old socialists. Felter gave him a third fifty, as a tip, though his own pocket-lining was perished.

Paid up, and left to his Sunday afternoon, he read poetry under the plane trees. From this north side of St James's Park, he could see the towers of Westminster. The lake was in the foreground, and a sunny expanse of lawn. Nothing in central London pleased him as much as this composition, but it was only possible to enjoy it on Sundays. Today, those streets which normally islanded the Park in traffic were closed. The

Mall, immediately behind him, was closed. From 8 a.m. till dusk, from Admiralty Arch to the Palace. He basked in old-fashioned silence, only disturbed by occasional parties of passing tourists. The tourists no longer bothered him; they brought money to the Government. And while they did that, if he had learned anything in his disappointing life, the Mall's pink perspective would be preserved, carless, every Sunday, for their cameras.

He loaded his pipe – regrettably, he held shares in this tobacco – and re-read the second-to-last stanza of Spender's poem:

> All the lessons learned, unlearnt;
> The young, who learned to read, now blind
> Their eyes with an archaic film:
> The peasant relapses to a stumbling tune
> Following the donkey's bray:
> These only remember to forget.

That had been written when socialism failed in Spain. Young Felter had met Stephen Spender once, in 1958, outside the Old Vic. He had asked the poet to speak for CND; and, not getting the answer he wanted, had lectured him about weak intellectualism, and denounced the socialist poets of the thirties.

Now they were a comfort to him, the chroniclers of that sweet belief in Struggle. These modern English – he was going to die among them – were less lucky than beaten Spain. There was no crude oppressor here to make resistance possible, no kit-set dictator for poets to attack with donkey metaphors. No poets.

He looked up from his book. He liked to watch the figures in his landscape. Some strolling Japanese were no longer in sight; a girl with a ball had moved slightly to the left. White birds seethed over morsels at the lakeside. It was a painting he could contemplate for hours; the work of some still-active abstract good, labouring in a silence commissioned by tourism.

Then . . . what was it? Perhaps the silence had dropped a semitone, or taken on weight. Fanciful descriptions, but the change was fact. The fact was heavy movement, and the sense of silence caving in from the direction of Admiralty Arch. Pushed down the Mall by traffic.

The upper branches of the plane trees were still in full sunlight; this was not dusk by any penny-pinching definition. The clock of the Horse Guards confirmed with four smart bells; Big Ben came lumbering after. And Felter was already on his way through the trees to the roadside, reeling to the only noise in England louder than tourist money.

Six starred green lorries of the American army rolled down the long tongue of the Mall. Running down Sunday, overriding the rules American-style, soldier-style, gangster-style. He looked down as they passed, more out of embarrassment than as a protest. He had done with sulky gestures.

At the end of the Mall, the convoy rounded the Victoria Monument and filed past the grimy front of Buckingham Palace.

All the same, he would write an angry letter.

2

Half-changed, having just got back, the Secretary to the Secretary bolted his breakfast, sitting at a Chinese table by the window of his bedroom. Outside, on the Mall, the rush-hour was well under way. The first clustering coach-parties were at the Palace Gate; there was no time for coffee. He slipped on his shoes and checked his face in a pier glass for smudges of egg, crumbs, teeth marks. A two-hundred-year-old Chinaman lurked nearby, in a temple of golden palms, waiting to gong his lateness with an ormolu hammer. But at one minute to eight he was already heading north, measuring his steps along the Chamber Corridor.

This part of the Palace was filled with Chinese junk, hauled up in trainloads when Victoria ransacked the Brighton Pavilion to furnish her new East Front. These broken cabinets in the Chamber Corridor had once displayed pieces of carved red lacquer, but small and valuable things had disappeared when the staff moved out. He passed bamboo chairs, now split and seatless; climbing-frames for rats. Still, there remained the ubiquitous yellow, birds-in-fruit-trees wallpaper, the fat buddhas, the slender guardians in grottoed fireplaces, the massive hanging lotus lights . . . and that most immovable ornament, Lady Bracken.

He saw her now, a tall shadow advancing rapidly from the north. She seemed to move faster every morning, trying to panic him into speeding up. But he knew he was on time. And if they did not meet, at exactly two minutes past eight, next to the cabinet built for George IV's baby service, it would not be his fault.

'Good morning, My Lady.'

'Good morning, Mr Vane.'

So they passed every day. After waking the Queen she returned to her room at the southern end of the Chamber Corridor. That meeting permeated his mornings: her piled white hair with its long supporting pins – the kanzashi – stabbing out at him, the frighteningly inept painted curlicues around the eyes, the sacrificial lust in her greeting, the rearguard, sandalwood scent-attack, shot from the folds of her shit-coloured gown as she swished away. There was nothing essentially oriental about the Queen's Lady-in-Waiting, though a lifetime in the East Front had had its effect on her hairstyle. She was an English exoticist, motivated by an entirely English, unspecific loathing.

Shortly after his meeting with her, the Secretary to the Secretary reached the end of the Chamber Corridor and entered the North-East Staircase. His office was at ground level, two floors below. On the first-floor landing, a breeze blew up from the Principal Corridor, the main thoroughfare of the East Front. Another window had been broken somewhere. There were vandals and tramps in the Palace. Straight ahead of him was the North Wing, the King's Corridor, giving access to the Royal Apartments. A shock-haired old woman was hurrying in his direction, but turned back when she saw him. Where had she been off to, still in her dressing gown?

At the bottom of the stairs, Vane entered the North Wing. He used the Privy Purse Passage, a gloomy conduit which took him eventually to his office. There, light prevailed, and an Italian modernism favoured by the old prince, Spanish Tony, in his renovating days. No antique wreckage distracted from a view of the garden; just a desk on a grey carpet, a moulded chair, an ashtray and a glass wall.

The room was already hot. It was a freakish, mutant September. After ringing for coffee, he pushed aside one of the glass panes and stepped out on to the terrace. Except for the noise of the traffic on Constitution Hill, it could have been a summer morning in the country. He stopped in the sunlight and closed his eyes. He could be young again, having woken from a country sleep. But it was useless to pretend; only time and cigarettes would mend him. And there was Christina to attend to, possibly the only person in the world this morning who felt worse than he did.

She was sitting on the terrace steps in a black evening dress, black hair hanging, head between her knees.

'Good morning, Doctor,' he called.

She gathered herself up and tramped over to him, let him push the hair away from her face. 'You look as though you slept in the lake,' he said. 'Lost your key?'

He held her by the shoulders. She leaned against him briefly, then broke away and walked towards the door.

'Thank God you're here anyway. For a minute I thought I'd have to listen to that fucking Scotsman.'

A kilted crock had stationed himself thirty feet away, under the windows of the Queen's Dining Room: her decrepit Royal Pipe Major, making wheezy preparations for the breakfast recital. He was a legacy of Victoria's taste that no one had ever dared question. Vane ushered Christina inside and shut the door behind them.

'Got any coffee, Teddy?' She flopped into the Italian chair and scowled at the garden.

'It's coming. Shouldn't you be upstairs, dispensing morning pills?'

'She won't take them.' Christina lit a cigarette. 'Bracken put her up to it. Some Union of Witches has denounced Western medicine again. Well, it cuts the cost of looking after her.'

Vane emptied the contents of some delivery bags on to his desk and started to sort through them. 'At least Bracken keeps her happy.'

'Keeps her frightened you mean. The members of this family have always been suckers for cranks. Where the fuck is that coffee?

'Were you at Harrow last night?' she asked a little later. 'How's Erika?'

'Fine. Ian starts college next month. He's reading already, in case he gets sick during the term. Listen, you don't have any plasma in your surgery at the moment do you? There's a package from the Consulate this morning. Unscheduled, but . . .'

Christina brightened. 'Does that mean we can have a party later?'

He wagged a finger. 'You know the rules, my love; no bliss without blood.'

'I'll bring it down after breakfast.'

'Good girl.' He slit an envelope, a rare informal letter to the Queen. Christina saw his eyebrows go up. 'Good God! This is from Michael Felter.'

'Who?'

'An old socialist. My father knew him. He's complaining about the Americans driving their trucks down the Mall on Sundays. It's very long.' He put the letter aside. 'Should keep Britannia amused for a couple of hours.'

Outside, the Royal Pipe Major started to warm up. He marched along the terrace when he played; every half-minute a sickening strangulated cat-squeal flared and died as he came closer to them and wheeled away. Christina stood up abruptly.

'Jesus Christ! Fuck! Fucking noise! Fucking servants! I don't have time to wait for the coffee.'

She walked to the door and opened it. A liveried footman, carrying a loaded tray, stepped into the room.

'If you don't mind, I'm trying to get out!' Christina pushed past him, and the tray went into his face.

The room was filled with the smell of wasted coffee. And from outside, the agony of sound.

Lady Bracken set before her mistress a single poached egg on a blue willow plate. Queen Britannia suppressed her disgust; she hated Chinese patterns. Why could she not have simple English flowers? Bracken produced a leafy twig from a compartment in her gown, and with a pair of kitchen scissors, snipped it over the Royal Breakfast.

'Fresh!' she proclaimed. 'And brim-full of iron. This'll set you right.'

'But I don't feel at all badly this morning, Bibi,' Britannia said meekly, watching woody foliage raining on to her plate, remembering sausages, white toast and thick-cut marmalade and the pretty monogrammed butter-pats of the past. 'And I do rather think it's my rooms give me the headaches.'

'Nonsense! This is the quietest suite in the Palace.'

'Yes . . . but do you know, after all these years I'm beginning to find it a little, well, small.' Bracken fetched a Waterford jug from a sideboard. The Queen ate her egg quickly, with involuntary faked enjoyment. 'After all, it isn't as though there weren't other suites empty. If I were to move to, well, the East Front, the Blue Suite, I'd certainly be much nearer to your rooms.'

She peeped hopefully at Bracken standing sternly by the chair, pouring mineral water into a glass.

'I enjoy the exercise,' said the Lady-in-Waiting, 'and no member of the family has ever lived in the Blue Suite. It is one of the Visitors' Apartments.'

'But we don't have visitors now. And it is so lovely, Bibi.'

Bracken banged the heavy jug down on the table and exhaled noisily. 'Well the great rooms are not what they used to be, Ma'am, since the cuts.'

Britannia pouted and sipped her water. Cuts had been mentioned, but she would not gratify Bibi with a response. There never had been, never could be any proven connection between her decision to promote the electronics industry and her subsequent hard times. Yet, God knew, things had changed after 1993, apart from her name.

She had wanted only to do her bit for the New Companies, to be a good stick, to be no better than the next man. Yet she had ended up something worse, held in special contempt. How else to explain the savagery of the bureaucrats – the Civil List cuts, the staff cuts, the power cuts?

Bibi had opposed the Britannia Box promotion, had called the name-change scandalous. But it had been the Government's wish. How could a Constitutional Monarch have refused them? Bibi had shaken her head. Poor dear Prince Anthony would not have stood for this nonsense, Bibi had said. She had predicted disaster. And she had been right.

Under the window, Old Malcolm wailed for

Britannia. She had not seen him for years, but she thought of him as a friend; undemanding, still coming out in all weathers, into his seventies now, but always there, with his plaintive music, the call to a lost cause. She imagined he saw visions of the Jacobite rebellion; once, Bracken had whispered of a rosary found near his room in the South Wing. Britannia smiled, and looked towards the far end of the big oval table. Tony's face had always been a picture when Malcolm played. How he had hated the sound of the pipes.

'And what would the Prince have thought of this moving business,' Bracken demanded, 'after you lived so long together in this part of the Palace?'

Britannia suspected sometimes that under the stern exterior of her Lady-in-Waiting was a core of pure malice. She held up her eggy plate for removal.

'But the Prince is dead, Bibi,' she said firmly.

Later in the morning, Vane opened a satchel marked for his attention by an official at the Consulate of Chipoquaqua. Inside was a single package, rubber-stamped in several places: BY DIPLOMATIC BAG. It was addressed: TO HER MAJESTY QUEEN BRITANNIA. A GIFT FROM THE DEMOCRATIC REPUBLIC OF CHIPOQUAQUA. Vane removed the outer covering and broke the seal of a wooden cigar box. He put his finger under the lid and raised a dusting of white powder to his tongue. Satisfied, he ran a flat paperknife across the surface of the contents, gathering a light harvest.

The cigar box was kept in a locked drawer. When he put it away, Vane brought two other items out on to his desk: an empty Fortnum and Mason tea caddy and an insulated bag of white plasma. He sealed the plasma inside the caddy, wrapped it, and addressed it: TO THE PRESIDENT OF THE DEMOCRATIC REPUBLIC OF

CHIPOQUAQUA. A GIFT FROM HER MAJESTY QUEEN BRITANNIA. Then he put it in the diplomatic satchel.

His morning's work over, he picked up his phone and rang the Palace switchboard.

'Vane here. Page the Queen's Physician for me would you?'

While he waited, he shook the powder from the knife on to a piece of black paper which he folded carefully to enclose the contents in a small square. He put it into his pocket, and the phone rang.

'Hello, Chris? Lunch in ten minutes? Fine.'

They ate in Soho, the American quarter; steak and Volnay '95 at John Wayne's, a fibreglass ranch interior, decked with ribboned American senior staff: Texan generals on leave from the European bases, military 'advisors' to the British Government. These people wallowed in the best places like sacred bison, bragging about the war that was coming, swapping cigars with English electronics tycoons.

Vane looked sourly around the room and sawed off a forkful of flesh.

'Doesn't the Home Office ask what you do with it all?'

Christina shrugged. 'I told them Britannia has a rare hereditary disease. What do they know? She doesn't cost them much now, anyway. At least the bastards can pay for some plasma every now and then.'

'Well, if this coke's good, we should get fifty grand each.'

'I can use it after last night. Car's totally fucked. That idiot Fox-Peeper . . .'

'Is he the MI6 man?'

'Yuh . . . offered to drive me home, and I woke up at dawn on Beachy Head. From the state of the suspension I'd say he drove cross-country . . .' She cocked her head, smiling at him. 'And your half goes . . . to Erika again?'

He nodded. 'Ian won't live six months if I don't find half a million. That's how it is now.'

'Ah, Teddy, you're so noble.' She went on smiling at him. The cold point of her shoe found the opening of his trouser-leg and slipped inside. 'Blue Bedroom after lunch?'

He grunted assent, his mouth full of blood and wine. So, good days began.

From the Privy Purse Passage they climbed, giggling a bit, to the first-floor landing, slipped past the entrance to the Royal Apartments and into the Principal Corridor. The sun, directly above the courtyard windows, laid short blocks of light on the carpet, gave shadows to the bodies of flies. Heat sucked out their old-age smell from wood and the fabric hangings. Vane's breakfast-time breeze had retreated to the upper air, working along the cornice and the choked crevices of picture frames. Dust rained perpetually. Christina leaned on him, and they crept southwards.

Halfway along the corridor they passed an open room, radiant yellow, with three window-lengths of sharp blue sky. A painted glass lotus-chandelier moved slightly on its foliated chain; this was where the weather had made its tentative invasion. Vane crossed to the middle window, a French door which had swung open. There were leaves on the carpet and a crisp-packet lodged in a porcelain pagoda.

At the door, he turned and called Christina over. He took her arm, and they stepped out between two dirty, fluted columns. On to the Royal Balcony.

Below them, at the Palace gate, someone shouted and pointed. Violence erupted as a party of new arrivals fought to get out of their coach. A rear window was smashed and from inside a voice called, *'Altesse! Votr' Altesse!'*

'They think you're the Queen, Chris,' said Vane. 'Why don't you give them a wave?'

Christina unbuttoned her jacket and showed them her tits. The crowd hissed with displeasure. Vane pulled her by the hair and bent her backwards over the parapet, kissing her savagely, watching the tourists howl at the railings.

'We'd better get inside,' he said. They shut the door behind them and he kissed her again, while the storm broke outside, raining Coke cans, cameras, Cornettos.

They moved on to the next room along the Corridor. Away from yellow to the Blue Sitting Room, from writhing Chinese painted bronze, to inlaid old-English satinwood. They shared a distaste for excess.

He sat near the window to prepare the coke, in sunlight filtered through figured silk. Out in the dark room – the walls were turquoise rather than blue – she struck poses beneath French flower paintings. She twined herself around a tall clock-pedestal, decorated with classical panels, and settled finally on a gilded chaise longue, surely the only modern woman who could look comfortable on those ramparts of period seduction. She cupped her neck in its terminal curve and stared at the ceiling, trailing a leg over the side.

'Coke,' she moaned, and closed her eyes.

No sign of life compromised her perfect obscenity. He crossed to her and knelt by her head. He put his hand into the hanging hair. His fingers touched the delicate skull, cradled it, lifted it to the spoon.

On from there to the Blue Bedroom. On to French Revolution silk for slow sex. The walls were made of Italian skies, landscapes, ruins.

They knew their way round that four-poster. He was good at his job, serviced her as well as anyone, to judge by the noise she made. And he got a weird satisfaction out of that, because she had plenty to compare him with.

Things were different with Erika.

Christina, cold as a doctor, had a doctor's power to heal.

On the painted pedestal, Father Time, glorified child-abuser, clipped cupid's porcelain wings. Above them a clock struck four, and in the next room Vane woke up, his mind still racing. How could that clock be working? The last Palace Clockwinder had died three years ago.

Waiting to decide to move, he peered over Christina's brown, sleep-expanded body. The bedroom door framed a view of the Blue Sitting Room; a section of wall, with the door to the Principal Corridor, a corner table with a vase, half of a painting above it. He isolated this group, considered its composition, colour, lighting. And when he had quite formalized it, flattened it, forgotten it, it broke up in front of his eyes.

When someone opened the door from the Principal Corridor, he broke up.

What a triumph for Bracken, to find them here like this! He ran, naked, to close off the bedroom before she emerged from behind the sitting-room door. But the bedroom door had sunk out of alignment, and jammed on the carpet, half open. He looked through the gap between the hinges, and saw her arm as she closed the outer door gently behind her. The care she took modified his panic. She was nervous too, and behaved like an intruder here.

She seemed to have moved off in the direction of the window. Her back would be to the bedroom. He decided to get a better look at her. It was a chance to catch her out with a bottle of methylated spirits, a book of male nudes, a gun. He crept to the edge of the door, and looked. He couldn't see her. He craned his neck, his body; put out an arm, a leg, and finally abandoned cover completely.

It was Britannia, not Bracken. The old woman, in a tattered white summer dress, was crouched at a dwarf bookcase behind the chaise longue, squinting at the titles on ancient spines. Her head was turned slightly away; he could have retreated immediately, but he remained in the open, biting his lip.

What would happen if she saw him? He couldn't imagine it, so he couldn't fear it. He believed that if she turned around now, he would be invisible to her. He had never suspected her of this power, this residue of divinity, which made it impossible, yes impossible, for a naked man to come into her presence.

But he lost his brief faith when she suddenly stood up. He jumped back behind the door and continued to watch her as she moved around the room, clutching the book she had selected. She took possession of the place, domesticated it, visiting in turn each of the satinwood treasures, delighting in them more than as mere works of art. He watched as she traced with her finger a world-famous inlay. She had been a child here.

He was ready to feel sorry for her, to admit that what had happened to her was a tragedy. To see wrecked royalty, unselfconscious amongst beauty, anybody, even Christina, might have felt a pang of nostalgia. He was ready to let pity contaminate his usual indifference to the Queen. But something about her forbade it.

He saw it most clearly after she had been standing for a few minutes at the window, watching the tourists. They were her last loyal subjects. But if the dreary facade of the Palace had turned out to be nothing more than a painted screen, if some men came one morning and dismantled it, and the visitors finally realized that the Monarchy was finished, they would cross it off their lists, and find something else to stare at. Yet, it appeared that they still meant something to Britannia. He saw a watery self-satisfaction in her eyes when she turned away from them. Did she cherish some misconception concerning them?

She sat down near the window and started to read. Vane crept back to bed; there was nothing to do but wait. Christina was still fast asleep. No, she would not feel any sympathetic pangs for Britannia. She had the medical facts. It was a simple enough case. The old bitch was mad.

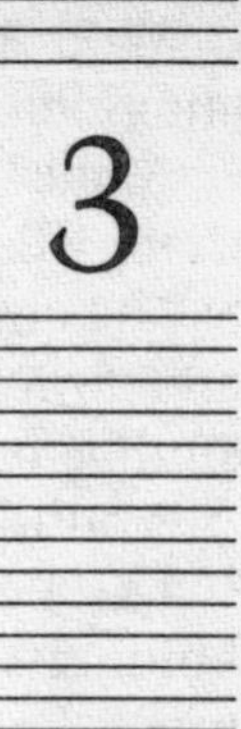

At the Golden Age arcade in Kings Cross, they had brought back old-style fruit machines. The nineties had been all aluminium facias, digital displays and credit cards. But the fathers of young gamblers still talked of the spinning drum, the row of cherries, the bar, and the rattle of metal money. The reintroduction of fruit machines to the arcade by the station was a success.

A fifteen-year-old boy, just in from the North, was putting the last of his money into one of the new machines. He had high hopes for London, and was celebrating his arrival with the first temptation that had come his way. His next was to be a session at McDonalds, but the prospects for real food were coming more and more to rest on the fall of the painted. He had three one-pound coins left to get back fifteen. He needed straight melons. But if he was to go down, to be ruined by the city in his first hour, at least the tragedy would have a witness. A man who looked a bit like a schoolteacher stood next to him, watching. The boy squared up to the machine, and fought it for his money. He had a natural flair for the nudge; he won on his last coin.

'Well done!' The stranger clapped him on the shoulder and asked him how much he had made.

'Made? I've not made anything, mate. Broke even, that's all.'

The question had soured his victory. He spoke curtly and wandered away. But the man would not be snubbed.

'You'll never get anywhere like that.'

The boy stopped. The man meant profit, not just holding your own in the city, but taking from it. He must be smarter than a teacher then. There was certainly a look about him that no teacher ever had, the look of people who know they're in control.

'Try that machine over there. I'm Peter, by the way.'

'Damon.'

'Just one coin, Damon. The second from the end.'

Twenty identical machines, side by side, all fixed at daylight robbery. Why this one, instead of another?

'I'll not risk more than one, mind.'

'You're not risking anything.' Peter smiled.

And Damon played of course. It was better than food anyway, watching the three drums go; more physical than filling up, waiting for the colour to stop. Click. Click. Click. Three green melons, for the second time in five minutes. Another fifteen pounds, and pure profit this time. He was richer than he'd ever been in his life.

'We should go now,' Peter said. 'The attendants don't like to see people winning.' As they walked towards the door, he explained. 'The machine hoards, but it has to pay out eventually. You watch for the punters who give up, or run out of money. If three people have played a machine without winning, you know it's primed. The staff are on the lookout too: they top it up and collect – that's their perks. But if you're smart, you get in before them. It's quite legal.'

Damon didn't respond. He mistrusted free advice, especially when it was good. They were out in the street now, and there was no reason to stay together. Damon had new money in his pocket; he was thinking of escape. Then this Peter started to talk to himself.

'Shall I stay for a McDonalds?' He squinted at the sky. Damon looked up with him to the red clock-tower of St Pancras Station. 'No, no . . . There isn't time. Business appointment at five . . .' He looked thoughtfully at Damon, as if wondering how to amuse him. 'D'you want to come back to my place for a bite? It's just around the corner.'

Damon fixed his gaze on a passing car. 'Got to meet some mates here now.'

'Ah.' Peter smiled briskly and handed him a small printed card.

P. Pounce. The Old Brewery, N.1.
Anguis Bicephalous

There was also a telephone number.

'Ring me,' said Peter Pounce. 'Any time. Look after yourself. Never go into an arcade with more than a pound, or come out with less than twenty. Well, I must be getting back. Goodbye, Damon.'

He walked away. Damon stared at the card. The word beginning with 'A' seemed to have one letter too few, or too many. The other word was too difficult to even think about. He looked up and, without knowing why, called out.

'Hold on then, mate. I'm coming now.'

They walked north-east from King's Cross through villainous streets of old warehouses, all hatchways open to catch any afternoon breeze. People sat on boxes out of doors, stretched themselves on loading docks, or stayed in the gutted interiors, grouped wherever an electric light had been rigged up. Some were on blankets or filthy settees; reading, scratching themselves over newspaper puzzles. Any television attracted squabbling mothers and their children. Teenagers clung together on the periphery of light. The men stayed in the streets with the dogs.

Damon recognized cooking smells, accents, facial types. There were Northerners here, his own people. People – but not living like people. A fat woman with a shaven child waddled towards them, singing in a little girl's voice, 'Yesterday, all my troubles seemed so far away.' A black man spread a handkerchief on the ground to display toys he had made from bits of old typewriters. Peter Pounce stopped to buy one.

'Is this the Waitings?' Damon asked, when they started off again. 'Where people wait for interviews.'

'How did you know?'

'My dad came here once, about ten years ago, when they stopped his dole. He got a letter saying there was no dole any more, 'cause everyone had a job.'

'Everyone does have a job, theoretically.'

Damon looked up at him. 'Here, Pete, are you a teacher?'

'I was. Tell me about your father.'

'They said they'd used his last giro to buy him shares in some big company at Swinthorpe, and that he had a job there. Only there's no such place.'

'It's one of the "dormant" New Companies,' said Pounce. 'It exists on paper, but it won't become operational until there's a demand for its product.'

'What sort of product?'

'Oh, penny-farthing bicycles perhaps. Something for which there never will be a demand. Anyway, your dad came to put his case in Whitehall. What happened?'

'He got sick while he was waiting and came home.

I'm not surprised, looking at this bloody place. Is that what you're doing, Pete? Are you waiting?'

Peter Pounce put his hand on Damon's shoulder. 'No, my love. I'm afraid I simply take.'

The Waitings finished abruptly at Regents Canal. At the point they came on to it, they were opposite a dirty brick building with five floors of boarded-up windows on either side of a high round chimney. At roof level, the chimney's brickwork became fancy. There was an ornamental parapet, and a huge green dome. Below the parapet were faded words, the name of a business, and its date, older than Damon could easily imagine. A long plank was lashed to the front of the chimney.

Peter Pounce called out, 'Watcher!' Damon was surprised by the strength of his voice. A ginger-haired boy popped out of the top of the chimney and waved. He disappeared and immediately the plank was lowered across the canal. Pounce stood back to let the guest go first. 'Welcome to the Old Brewery,' he said.

They entered by a door in the base of the chimney and climbed up inside it, on a spiral staircase. There was light from long slits cut into the wall. At the top landing, a ladder continued on up to the chimney's mouth, where the ginger-haired boy perched, peering down at Damon.

'Don't bring the bridge up, Watcher,' Pounce called, 'Mr Vane will be here soon.'

Watcher didn't respond, but Pounce seemed satisfied and went on into the main part of the building.

When Damon first saw the Common Room, and the silent boys at work under a giant clock, he was ready to kick Pounce in the balls if that was what it took to get away. But, while keeping that as an option, he could not ignore the other thing, the powerfully delicious smell of hot food, ready for eating.

He counted twelve boys, mostly his own age, sitting around a long wooden table. It was the big room's only piece of furniture, apart from some chairs by a fireplace. The only light came from the table; each of the workers had his own electric lamp. They were isolated on a floor of polished boards. Above them a four-faced station clock was suspended from the interior of the dome. Damon was fascinated by that black hole; strips of torn lining material waved in its depths, a rough system of support-beams was amplified in mad shadow by the lamps on the table below. The dome amplified Damon's foreboding.

'It looks very neat from outside,' said Pounce, 'but the Victorians weren't bothered about what their workers had to see.'

'You could take those beams out,' said Damon, 'and put in supports to fit the shape of the dome.' He spoke almost to himself, out of an understanding he barely recognized. Pounce was delighted.

'Ah, there is an English craftsman in you, Damon.'

'My grandad was an engineer. He helped build an oil rig.'

'Did he now?' Pounce smiled at him. 'Come on, let me show you my bedroom.'

It was at the top corner of the building. The bed itself occupied the whole of a large alcove. Pounce flung himself down on it as soon as they arrived.

'Come and have a look,' he said excitedly.

Damon sat on the bed and edged a little way into the alcove. It jutted out over the canal. From a window above Pounce's pillow he saw a long stretch of steely water. He counted five bridges.

'They had a winch up here in the old days,' said Pounce. 'They hauled the grain off the barges direct, brought it up through the floor on pallets. There's still a trapdoor under the bed.'

Damon shifted uneasily, and Pounce playfully touched his leg. 'Don't worry, it's bolted from underneath.' He gazed down at the canal, forgetting to remove his hand. 'It's lovely. I only wish a barge, loaded with sacks, would come past every now and then.'

Peter Pounce stood up. 'Well, let's get back to the Common Room. It's almost dinner time.'

The boys at the table were still working silently. The minute hand clicked over their heads. Nobody looked up.

'Five-twenty, boys.' Pounce walked over to the table and stood behind two boys who looked like brothers. 'Mr Vane been through yet, Macrobe?'

The elder boy shook his head. Close up, Damon could see that the top of the table was covered by a mirror. Using thin-stemmed funnels, the boys filled tiny glass capsules from bottles of white powder. If any precious crystals escaped, they found them on the mirror, and retrieved them with the tips of their fingers.

Pounce watched the younger of the two brothers for a minute. He was no more than eight or nine, and worked slowly, with his tongue sticking out between his lips. When he finished with one capsule, his master bent down and whispered to him. The little boy flushed with pleasure. Then Pounce straightened up and turned to Damon, saying something about a gym.

They had to go down a floor. From a window on the stairs, Damon saw the landscape at the back of the brewery. A roadless tract of rubble, a moon-city of partially demolished tower-blocks and craters. There were places like this in his home town. He realized that the brewery was isolated between this wasteland and the canal. There was the drawbridge, but when that was up, the building was completely cut off.

He did not want to see the gym. There had to be one;

work and sport always went together. He looked sourly at a room filled with implements of torture he recognized from school. Meanwhile, Pounce explained that he hoped eventually to install a swimming pool on the ground floor.

'Do you like sport, Damon?'

Do you like sport Damon? Would you like something to eat, Damon? Why don't you sit down here, Damon? All the long looks and soft enquiries of soppy-eyed men who wanted you to go home with them. It had started when he was twelve. Strangers had started to care for him, just at the time his family became indifferent. Other boys were jealous, and girls giggled. But if he was rude to the men, he always regretted it.

'No, I fuckin' hate sport as a matter of fact.'

Peter Pounce laughed and touched him again. 'So do I. So do I. But I like to watch. Come on, why don't you try the horse?'

Macrobe came into the gym and announced that the man called Vane had arrived upstairs.

'About time,' said Pounce. 'Show him into my office, will you love . . . Oh, and tell whoever's carving tonight to give your little brother an extra slice. He's done well on his first day.'

'The little one is called Microbe,' Pounce explained when the messenger had gone, 'so the big one is Macrobe, d'you see? They're new here. Actually their names are Mike and Mack, but I could never remember which was which.' He turned abruptly and started to walk towards the door. 'And now, I have business upstairs. Try to amuse yourself here while the boys get the Common Room ready for dinner. We eat at six, sharp.'

Damon watched him recross the floor of the gym. A dainty walker, a weedy body, not old and not young. The sort of person you might pinch ten quid from. So how come those boys upstairs worked for him like slaves?

There were some balls lying around on the floor of the gym: a football and, next to it, one slightly larger, leather-skinned. He gave this ball a sharp kick and jumped back, cursing and in pain. The ball rolled over once and wobbled a bit. He stared at it for a second in disbelief, then took his revenge on the weaker ball. He banged it against the wall and when it came back he banged it in again. He caught it with the top of his foot, and sent it on a high curve to the other end of the room. He chased it, laughing out loud, and scooped it up before it stopped bouncing, juggling it from one foot to the other until his chest hurt . . . and he remembered what Peter Pounce had said about liking to watch. He turned round quickly and looked at the entrance to the stairs. Nobody was there, but the ball had rolled away, and he felt slightly dizzy. What he really needed was food.

The Common Room was transformed. The factory had disappeared, the mirror was gone. The work lamps had been rearranged down the centre of the table and twelve places were set. There were jugs of apple juice and long loaves of bread. Boys in aprons arrived from another part of the building with pots of steaming soup. Damon waited by the empty fireplace, where the workers were gathering, filtering back from somewhere, changed for dinner.

They had been wearing grey tracksuits before. Now they were groomed for evening, in black trousers and white shirts, hair slicked back. Peter Pounce came into the room with another, much younger man – this must be Vane – who chatted to the boys for a few minutes then left. After that they took their places for dinner. Pounce sat next to the boy at the head. Damon was given a place near the other end, next to Microbe. Macrobe sat opposite, and the ginger-haired boy scowled at the bottom of the table. Nobody spoke.

Although Damon had never before shared a table with so many boys, he knew by instinct how to behave. As soon as he sat down he grabbed the nearest loaf of bread. But Macrobe kicked him under the table. 'Put it down, stupid. Grace comes first.'

'Who's she then?'

Microbe giggled. Then the boy at the top of the table said something, and after that everyone started talking, and the soup was handed round. This time Macrobe got the loaf first.

Soup and hot bread, with roast beef to follow, roast potatoes, peas, cabbage (he left that), and something called Yorkshire pudding, which he had never come across in his fifteen years of Yorkshire life. Apple crumble, ice-cream with chocolate sauce. Then the plates were cleared away, and two kitchen boys staggered in with a barrel of beer. The diners cheered, and banged their glasses on the table. But when Peter Pounce stood up, they shut up, and looked at him. What did they see there, Damon wondered? What authority did they hear when this schoolteacher spoke?

'Just before they serve the beer, a word with you my loves. You must get sick of hearing me say it, but I want you to be careful tonight. Most of you will be at the Electronics Ball, at Grosvenor House, and there won't be many Americans about. But wherever you are, in the Kings Road or St James's, in a club, a restaurant or a casino, don't try to sell to Americans!

'The use of drugs is a capital offence in the American army. Their military police shot your friend Spicer in the back. Stay away from them. Stay away from Soho. Sell to the rich English. They use the most and they pay the most.'

*

Everyone was given a pint, except for Microbe who stayed with apple juice. As the boys drank, their conversation got louder. Damon did not want to join in, but he wanted to understand what was said. Nobody explained anything. He was left in the dark, a second-class citizen, like the contented junior at his side. But Damon was not content. And when he had drunk most of his pint, he was ready to break out of the ghetto.

Watcher and Macrobe were talking together, so Damon reached over Macrobe's head and tugged the arm of the next boy.

'Hey mate.' He gestured with his glass to the other end of the table. 'He's a bit of a queer isn't he, that Pounce bloke?'

The boy looked away. Perhaps he hadn't heard. Perhaps they had a different word in London. He swallowed another mouthful of beer and addressed his neighbours at large.

'That's right isn't it boys? He takes it up the arse, that Peter Pounce?'

The effect was the same as before. Macrobe and Watcher glanced at him when he spoke, then went back to their conversation. Only the little boy next to him looked up from his glass of apple juice, and stared at Damon with big eyes. Damon bent down and spoke quietly. 'Hey littl'un. Why don't you ask your brother if you'll have to be a bum boy like him when you grow up?'

Microbe looked puzzled. Macrobe leaned across the table and spoke to him.

'Do you remember what Peter told you, Mikey, about the white powder.'

Microbe nodded solemnly and recited, 'The white powder is only good for the rich. If poor people like us take it, it poisons us, and we go mad.'

Macrobe nodded and looked at Watcher with a satisfied smile. 'He'll be all right,' the ginger-haired boy affirmed.

When the boys started to sing, and sway from side to side, Damon knew he had to leave. No one seemed concerned when he got up from the table. He made it to the chimney door and on to the stairs, inadequately lit now by strips of a pink sunset. Halfway down, stumbling in the bad light, he heard Pounce calling to him from the top landing. The voice was enquiring, but not threatening. Damon hurried on to the floor of the chimney and stopped. As far as he could tell, there was no one on the stairs behind him. He could still hear faint singing from the Common Room. At this depth there was no light at all. He groped along the wall for the outside door. He found it, and opened it.

The drawbridge was up, blocking the path. No wonder Pounce hadn't been worried. Damon realized he had run to the bottom of a well. He stared stupidly at the black space where the door should have been, trying to think of something to say when he got back upstairs. He had been looking for the toilet. It didn't matter how implausible.

Then two thin lines of evening light appeared on the chimney wall, and expanded towards each other as the drawbridge fell away. He didn't ask why; he scrambled out on to the bridge while it was still high above the opposite bank. He clung to it until he could stand, then ran to the end and jumped off into the sulphurous streets of the Waitings, heading for Kings Cross and the Golden Age.

At ten o'clock the boys went off to work. From the top of the chimney Peter Pounce watched them file across the drawbridge, then put his hand to the winch. But he decided to leave the plank down. He would never prevent a boy from leaving, or from coming back.

He had learned a lot. On nights like these, with order functioning, the wide eccentric roof of his domain spread below him, there was a case for self-congratulation. But it was their achievement, not his; their energy, stage by stage pulling this heap of rotting Victorian brickwork back into life. In the staff room, that charnel-house, he would have sneered at the idea. A secondary-level history hack with redundancy appeals pending. Thank God the appeals had failed, sparing him for renovation.

He would never have believed how hard they could work, what genius youth could spare for a temporary refuge. Fletcher, for example, who designed and built his office. His feelings had been very mixed when it was finally time for Fletcher to go. Now, the great green hump of the dome swarmed up in the darkness, demanding attention, and he hoped he had not lost Damon for good.

He turned back to the wide view past the canal. On the roofs of the Waitings figures moved against the glare from Kings Cross; people and animals, coming up for air. And beyond King's Cross, the superabundant halo of the West End, the tawdry beacon of centuries. He hoped he had not lost Damon for good.

He sweated in his bed above the canal. A woman shouted some words of abuse and there was a splash. The Waitings seethed on these hot nights. He relied on transport by water, but the system had broken down. The bargemen were on strike, their horses wandered off into the Waitings and were butchered for meat. The bargemen said the thing in the water would sink them. It looked small on the surface but was broad below, and it could move into any channel by which he might try to escape.

He got up and dressed. He had to reassure himself before he would sleep.

Streetlights provided the only electricity supply to the Waitings. Parasitic cables hung from the tall poles, siphoning power into derelict warehouses, and the streets were dark except for the packing-case fires of the truly homeless. These fires signalled gatherings of beggars and drunks, and Peter Pounce avoided them when he went out at night. There were alleys of dogs to be avoided too, and those upper windows where the risk was greatest of a sudden piss-pot deluge . . .

It was nearly eleven by St Pancras clock when he got to the Golden Age. Light beat from every surface, in every colour. Excessive and dangerous, aggravated by mirrors and shiny machines, it stalked the open spaces for something soft to eat, and found human flesh.

The skins of young gamblers could take it. But Peter Pounce suffered in front of those mirrors. His confidence was shaken by the age-and-ugliness-enhancing qualities of fluorescent light. At night, the glare was so fierce that he could not function, could not even approach the boys. So he stayed away. That was when Miss Gunsmoke had the place to himself.

He was Peter Pounce's rival in the Golden Age. A flashy bastard with American pretensions, notably a pair of tooled calfskin cowboy boots that always impressed the boys.

The rivals had never made more than eye-contact, but they knew each other's habits like cell-mates. Miss Gunsmoke's skin was indifferent to fluorescent light. He was young, still in his twenties, and brown, smooth. He could filch a boy from under Peter Pounce's nose by coming on like a dream buddy, a real big brother. And he gave them nothing. Nothing. In a few days, Pounce would see them back in the Cross, fuddled with dope and fucked. He either salvaged what he could, or gave Miss Gunsmoke the satisfaction of knowing that, yet again, the pleasure had been all his.

When he got to the Golden Age it was already too late. He wanted to walk out at once, to go somewhere dark and break something. But he knew his retreat would add to Miss Gunsmoke's pleasure. As it was, the Kings Cross cowboy might be unaware that this boy he had just picked up was a fugitive from the brewery. Pounce took a pretended interest in the game of some other, less attractive boy, and hoped that Damon would keep his mouth shut.

But Damon had just made his second London friend that day, and he had used his new trick to win another fifteen pounds. As he shovelled the money into his pocket, he saw Peter Pounce at the other end of the room. He was too happy to let his bad behaviour stand between them. He came bouncing up, certain of his ability to make everything right.

'Hey Pete, just cleaned up again y'know. Great system that!'

Pounce looked at the stupid, grinning boy and the muscles in his own face tightened.

'Why don't you come back, Damon? There are other things I can teach you.'

'Oh yeah, well . . . I met this mate of mine . . .' He gestured towards Miss Gunsmoke, discreetly busy in the background, lighting a cigarette, 'and he's got a bike so . . . we're going for a ride.'

Pounce nodded. Damon's shamelessness only added to his charm.

4

Things were different with Erika.

Christina catered to her own needs. And though her needs were uniformly vile, she was proud of her self-sufficiency. If she gave to a man, she gave involuntarily, like a fancy horse pissing in a parade. She was similar to most of the girls Edward had known. But Erika's affections were not inhibited by pride.

Christina avoided commitment to others; Erika had a teenage son who was dying of leukaemia.

Christina lived in other people's flats; Erika had a home for Edward to go to.

He left the brewery just before six, and walked through the Waitings to Kings Cross. At times like these, when his briefcase was stuffed with two thousand fifty-pound notes, he valued the untouchability of lackeys. A pressed suit was armour here, where, by rights, they should have killed him for his tiepin. Had respect for the establishment survived even the New Companies rip-off? Or was it apathy that preserved this system, this government – people's reluctance to endorse change when every change so far had been for the worse? Or then again it might be the sweet expectation of nuclear attack, and the consolation that on that day, those double-crossing bastards in Whitehall would burn with the rest.

He took the Metropolitan Line from Kings Cross to Harrow, strolled down wide, garden streets to the half-timbered doll's house where a man he had never met once lived with a pretty young wife. He let himself in, left his briefcase in the hall, and walked through to the back lawn.

Erika was by the fence, bent over some tiny concern among the flowers, buttocks thrust freely into the air. She stood to kiss him, wiping peaty fingers on her canvas trousers. 'You're late. Aren't you?'

'Yes . . . Sorry. Britannia held me up. Had a good day?'

'The pulsatilla is bad this year.' She smiled diffidently. He watched her readjust to accommodate his presence. She was alone here all day, a strong woman coping with weakness in the life around her. He wanted to share the responsibility, to be trusted with it, to meet it.

'Now.' She took his arm and marched him across to a white garden table. 'You will sit down, and I will bring you a beer.'

She went inside. He luxuriated in the domesticity, the quiet suburban evening, the shadows of clipped shrubs creeping across the lawn. The rear gable of the house needed painting. There was a crack in the window of Ian's room. Edward had a list of things that needed doing . . . when this place became his home . . . when he and Erika were married . . . after Ian's operation. There would be fresh paint on everything then.

Erika was a German native, from farming country near the Czech border. She had come to England as a tourist in 1982, and had stayed. A twenty-year-old girl from the European frontline, she had preferred to marry English security. He was a City man, a solid earner, a good father to her son. Then he had died. He developed acute leukaemia and died in a matter of months. That was in 1988. In 1989 the map of Europe changed. The front line lurched seven hundred miles westward. Capitalism reeled, and Erika lost her family.

Ian inherited the disease. It first manifested itself when he was twelve. He responded well to chemotherapy, but the remissions never lasted. When he was fifteen, doctors pronounced that only a bone-marrow transplant would save him. It took a year from then to locate a compatible donor; he was asking half a million pounds.

Erika did not have the money. And after her husband's illness, she had been unable to find medical insurance. Ian's English grandparents did their best, but the New Company in which they held shares had been slow. They were good Conservatives, but they lamented the National Health Service when they learned that their boy had less than two years to live.

Erika came out of the house with a tray and two bottles of beer. An amiable country hostess in a close-fitting skirt and heels, blonde hair pulled back from the fleshy face; excitingly German, to please the tourists. He believed his presence comforted her at least, re-established a pattern of family evenings – a man to feed, to ignore, to bicker and sleep with.

'We have sausage for dinner.' After twenty years, her accent still shocked the Harrow shrubbery. 'But Ian will not eat it. I am always having to buy some new gunk.'

'Gunk!' Edward laughed. There were these constant reminders of the other Englishman in her life. He had bought this house, sat at this table, loved this woman . . . But he had left it to someone else to save his son. 'Erika, I've got another fifty thousand. It's in my briefcase.'

'That's marvellous, Edward!' She was never prepared for it. She flushed deeply, became girlish, studied the design on the tray. 'But I suspect you of terrible crimes. Won't you tell me how you earn this money?'

He leaned back, enjoying it, and put a finger to his nose.

Ian stayed in his room, reading, till Erika called him for dinner. She waited for him at the foot of the stairs, and Edward, coming in from the garden, found them wrestling in the hall. Ian was wriggling and laughing while his mother got him into a half-nelson and tried to bring her hand into contact with his forehead.

'Don't tell me you haven't got a temperature!' she shouted. 'Look how red you are. Edward, isn't he red?'

Ian broke away and ran out of the house. Edward thought he had never seen a healthier boy. But six months ago, he remembered, Ian had been off school for eight weeks.

'He's working too hard for this damn university!' She stood at the front door, arms akimbo, looking up and down the street. Ian was not in sight.

'No one ever said that of a student before!' Edward kissed the back of her neck, put his arms round her waist, and felt her relax against him.

'Oooh Edward, daarling, that feels so goood . . .' It was Ian, standing behind them with a look of pantomime rapture on his face. Erika squealed with rage and lunged at him.

But after dinner – a jolly meal, boisterously

administered by Erika in her big kitchen – she was ready to relax, to let Edward assure her that it was all right for Ian to visit friends when the washing-up was done, ready for T.V. and chocolates, and Palace gossip.

On the news, there was a report from the Tenth Electronics Ball. It was the social event of the year, staged at Grosvenor House by the most successul New Company. Those who could afford to buy shares had been immensely enriched. All except the Queen, whose shares belonged in fact to the Government . . .

The Electronics Company owed its success to the Britannia Box, a product so advanced that ten years after its spectacular debut foreign technicians still scratched their heads over it. Those early days were commemorated tonight with a screening of the advertisement which had first proclaimed Britain's new industrial confidence.

It started with a close-up of the Queen's face in profile; soft-focus but unmistakable. Fireworks music played. Then the shot lengthened slowly, to reveal her as Britannia, with helmet and trident and Union Jack shield. By video effects the colours in the shield began to pulsate and send out flashes of red, white and blue lightning, while the figure of Britannia hardened into silhouette. The result, presented with a final rousing chord, was an image familiar now all over the capitalist world – the emblem affixed to the facia of every Britannia Box.

Erika, stretched out on the sofa, popped a chocolate into her mouth. 'It's a shame if everything you tell me about her is true. Will she be at the ball tonight?'

'Good God, no! She'd give them a terrible fright.' He was in the armchair. Things were fairly polite at this stage of the evening, before Ian was safely in bed.

'And what about you?' Erika did not look away from the television, 'Why aren't you there?'

He rolled his chocolate wrapper into a pellet and flicked it at her. 'I had a date with a hausfrau.'

She laughed silently. He could see the side of her face – the motion of the jaw as she ruminated over a hard centre, a few long strands that had escaped the discipline of her hairband.

'Christina is going?' she said.

'Oh yes . . . I should think so.'

'She is very beautiful. It would be worth going just to see her looking her best.'

'I see her every day. And she lives in evening clothes.' He would have liked to see more of Erika's face than that bluff unblemished cheek. But even then it would be impossible to tell if she suspected him and Christina, if she was worried by the suspicion, or knew she had no cause to be. There was only one sure way of reaching Erika, and sitting close like this through hours of television became a torture for him.

At ten-thirty the front door banged and they heard Ian thumping up the stairs. Erika roused herself, and shouted in the direction of the hall. 'Hey! Mister! Bed for you now please.'

Ian ignored her, or didn't hear, and after a while the muffled thump of rock music filtered from the top of the house. Erika sighed and shifted on the sofa.

'Oh well, that's it. Now he locks himself in his room with his joints and his American music, and swears at me if I try to reason with him. So, I couldn't care less. At least he won't dare to come downstairs. Why don't you sit here with me now, Edward?'

Between that discreet invitation, and the moment next morning when Edward left her to go to work, this protector of plants and sick children revealed herself a porno stuntwoman, a suburban anthropophagist, a rotting Rhine fish. He had been amazed, was amazed every night, to encounter the onslaught, the punitive enthusiasm of her lovemaking. No schoolfriend of his sister had fucked like this widow. No one he had known before, no self-conscious student-union slut, or ball-breaking fox huntress, shagged at a county soirée – no cool Christina had ever worked him, wanted him, trembled under his hand like Erika. And in the absence of other certain signs of it, he took this to be her expression of love.

The footman hovered with cream for Christina's morning coffee. She waved him away.

'Don't you ever get *sick* of sex though?'

Edward's hand shook when he lit his cigarette; this morning he was ready to take the question seriously.

'I mean, it brings you into contact with such utter shits. And they're always popping up afterwards. The Ball gets more gruesome every year. Last night was like a preview at a gallery in hell.'

'Was Fox-Peeper there?'

'Yes, odious creep. They've got him investigating people's sex lives at the M.I. Every time I had my eye on a dishy man, he came up behind me and whispered the name of some foul disease.' She drank her coffee and glared out through the glass wall at the trees. 'D'you know, I bought some coke from the tiniest boy last night. He looked a perfect angel, but wouldn't give an inch on the price. I should've taken some out of that kilo yesterday. There were dozens of these kids at the Ball, pushing dope to the morons; they were making an unbelievable profit . . . Oh, and there was a death.'

'A murder?'

'No. The Member for Islington choked on a fishbone. Fat bastard. You should've heard the noise he made!'

Outside, the Royal Pipe Major began with a slow march for those who had made it to a new day.

Later, the Secretary to the Secretary received one of his infrequent calls to attend the Queen in her study. Regular daily visits were a thing of the past, of the busy time when Sir Hugh Trafalgar had been the last full Secretary. Sir Hugh left, under Home Office pressure, when he objected to the changing of the Queen's name and the Britannia Box advertisement. The Queen had retaliated by refusing to countenance a successor. So the post had been left vacant, a painless early victory for the Government in its campaign to rationalize Palace staff.

Vane slicked down his hair, gargled with throat-stripper and took the lift from the Garden Entrance, near his office, to the King's Corridor. He knocked once on the door of the royal study, and entered. Britannia, wearing her darned morning twinset, was seated at her desk in the bay window. Ranks of framed photographs left only a polished central strip of the surface in front of her. Old friends and family, facing away from the visitor's idle gaze. She had lost one son to the rubber parlours of Sydney, an elderly daughter was ranching in Peru, the others had fled to places unknown and stayed there or died. As Vane approached, the Queen reached out and retrieved a picture which had strayed to the back.

'Charlie Boy,' she cooed, 'how did you get over there? Come back where mum can keep an eye on you.'

Charlie Boy – Vane tried to picture him – occupied a large frame, replaced now where Britannia could look at it, as if it were a mirror.

When her secretary was positioned in front of the desk, Britannia looked up and smiled. 'Now, Mr Vane, I wonder if you wouldn't mind making your entrance again. This time, rattle the door handle instead of knocking. Would you be so kind?'

He went out into the corridor, closed the door behind

him and rattled its handle before re-entering. He crossed to the desk, where the Queen, having put on a pair of heavy glasses, was reading a letter. When she saw him, she put the letter aside.

'Ah, good morning Mr Vane. How are you today?'

'Very well, ma'am.' He inclined his head deferentially. 'And you, ma'am?'

'I'm a little bothered, Mr Vane. But do take a seat.'

He sat down opposite her. While he had been rattling the door handle she had snapped into one of her brisk, capable moods; throwbacks from days when she had been credited with understanding if not the right to act upon it. Now, without even a puppet's chance for self-assertion, she could still do a wicked impression of her former style. It was difficult to banish respect for those businesslike glasses, whenever some ghost of a duty brought them into use. Vane could guess what had set her off this time.

'This letter,' she picked it up again, 'this name, Michael Felter. I can't quite put my finger on it. He's known to us in some way . . .'

'He was a public figure once, ma'am, in the 1960s; an anti-nuclear campaigner, and a socialist politician.'

'The socialists!' Britannia laughed merrily. 'Ah, yes. They were very severe about Kings and Queens. They didn't approve at all, not at all.' She wagged a finger at him. 'But it was the other lot who dished us in the end, eh, Mr Vane? And not for a principle, not for a principle mind, but a penny!'

She took off her glasses and put them on the desk. Rubbing her eyes, she leaned back and gazed at the ceiling, smiling, evidently pleased with her little outburst. Mad. Mad. Mad.

'He was also a friend of my father,' Vane said hesitantly. Was she still listening? Yes, she came back to him from the ceiling with a calm affectionate look.

'Your dear father . . . The Prince was very fond of him. He wrote a book, didn't he? What was it about now?'

'Conservation, ma'am.'

'Of course. Conservation. Environmental policy. Prince Anthony was very enthusiastic. I'm sure he felt your father deserved more attention.' She had slipped away again, out of focus, not seeing him any more. Seeing his father, probably.

'They were good men, Mr Vane. Men of great vision.'

While she blathered on, he looked around the room. Well-kept, but small by Palace standards; an old lady's room. He supposed it suited her. Nothing there to interest him though, except near the desk, a display case containing some gold coins, each perforated, and threaded with a piece of rotten ribbon. He could never remember what they were called. They were handed out to scrofula sufferers after the King had cured them with the touch of his fingers. How medicine had deteriorated. The practice went out with the Stuarts.

'I do not think you have inherited your father's philanthropic nature, Mr Vane.' Britannia must have noticed his boredom. She was toying with her glasses and studying him.

He flushed. Philanthropic nature was one way of putting it. He had always thought it was woolly thinking that he had failed to inherit from his father.

'I would admit that my impulses to good are less . . . general than his.'

The Queen was amused. 'And more likely to have effect, eh, Mr Vane? I hope so. It's getting harder to do anything for others.'

She rested a finger against her cheek, pulling down the skin from her eyes. She never wore makeup now; when her reading-glasses went on again, he watched the mottled magnified crows-feet reforming. She still wanted to talk about Michael Felter's letter.

'I think he must be the first socialist to remind me that I am still the leader of the British people.' They both laughed, not too heartily, at Felter's optimism. But then the Queen began to fidget, and said, very tentatively. 'I don't suppose there is . . . anything we can . . . do?'

Vane was appalled. What did she mean? He spoke quickly, to pre-empt his embarrassment. 'I'm afraid not, ma'am. The Americans have told the Department of the Environment that they need the use of the Mall on Sundays. There is to be an escalation of arms shipments to France, and the convoys must come through London. The DoE advises that the situation . . .'

'Yes yes, of course, Mr Vane . . . I'm sorry . . Of course.' The Queen had caught his panic. She knew she had upset everything by her audacity. She was sorry. She was sorry. She took off her silly glasses and tried to shuffle Felter's offending letter out of sight. As she did so, she knocked over some photographs. Vane got a good look at Charlie Boy; he had won the Derby in 1991.

'Well then, Mr Vane.' Britannia giggled nervously. 'I suppose you'd better write to Mr Felter and tell him that being the head of the British people does not give one the right to say what happens in one's own front yard!'

'Very well, ma'am.'

After that, he was dismissed. But as he walked away, she spoke again. 'Oh, Mr Vane.' He turned. 'I wonder if, all the same, you might remain facing me until you have left the room.'

After the Secretary to the Secretary had left her, Britannia remained slumped in her chair, sulking like a child. She had a sense of anti-climax. The day's business was over, and shortly the study clock would announce the first of many hours left till bedtime, the first of many hourly visits from one or other of her two attendants. She called them the Royal Hounds. If she was lucky, the official physician would be on duty; the girl, Christina. A Home Office plant, but acceptable, principally because of her utter indifference to her job.

But at the eleventh and final chime of the study clock, she became certain that her luck was out. She could feel the chill of approaching evil, the real danger to Royal health, its unofficial guardian: the gargoyle, the Witch-in-Waiting, Bracken. Britannia saw her in a vision, coming closer, consuming the Chamber Corridor with a tall glass of blended spinach in her hand. She had reached the North-East Stairs. Could the slap of her descending slippers be heard even at this distance? She was closer then, blocking the light in the King's Corridor, the kanzashi jutting like nails from her head, bearing down on the study with a dish of hot sucking entrails.

'Aaargh!' The Queen's hands were round her own throat. 'Tony! Help me! Save me!'

But she would have to save herself. Frantically she fished under the desk for her shoes, jammed them on, and hurried next door to her bedroom. A few seconds later, she heard Bracken rattle the handle of the study door, then enter. At that moment, Britannia escaped from the bedroom into the corridor. Not daring to risk the lift, she crept downstairs to the gloomy Garden Entrance and opened one of the big outside doors. Then she turned back into the Palace, heading west.

She took refuge in the West Wing, where the real splendour began, and the real desolation; where no one lived, or came for any reason, now that the staff were gone, and the suite of State Apartments had lost its place in the nation's life.

The State Apartments were on the first floor,

reached at this north end by the Ministers' Staircase, a funnel of ochreous light with a huge filthy window. By the stairs, Britannia peered back towards the Garden Entrance, listened for the slap of Bracken's Chinese slippers. There was no sign or sound of pursuit. But she could not be too careful; she climbed the first few steps, making clear footprints in the layered dust on the carpet, then descended, treading in the same marks, and began her real journey across the West Front, using its great dark ground-floor thoroughfare, the Marble Hall.

A two hundred-foot-long aisle of white columns with a mildewed scarlet carpet. And pictures that frightened her; this was a gallery of the Blood, the German line. The handsome Duke of Saxe-Coburg Gotha, a Princess of Hohenlohe-Langenburg, an early George, a Leopold of Belgium, a Leopold of Brabant, a Victoire of Nemours (pretty thing in ringlets), a Victoria of Kent (bonnetted frump), and the Winterhalter *them*: V and A, the high-water mark. He in green uniform, the balding bewhiskered husband. She crimson-swathed, little-mouthed, unseeing. Disgraced Britannia fled beneath them. And past their silly son, Bertie's bust, on a porphyry pedestal cut from a Carthaginian temple. Even he had kept his authority here, had never fled from servants down rotting red carpets. And what would that other night-clubbing King think of his Palace now, who had schemed away his credit to build it?

Halfway along the Marble Hall: the Grand Entrance from the Quadrangle. The guests had passed through here to functions in the State Apartments, anxious for a glimpse of her. Now she hurried on to the southern end of the Hall, anxious to forget. She entered a small room, once part of the Royal Library, then a breakfast room, now a shed of ransacked cabinets. Next, the former Household Dining Room, simple and spacious, with long windows onto the West Terrace. As she passed in front of them she did not notice her old friend Malcolm, the morning piper, leaning on the parapet outside, with his back to the wild West Lawn.

When he saw her his white brow twitched, he stuck out his beard, then nodded with satisfaction.

'Aye, theer she goes. Off tae her wee kirk. But theer's nae comfaert in Sass'nach relugion, lassie. It's been a lang time, but yeer comin' back tae us noo . . .'

Christianity had never played a large part in Palace life. The occupants, who protected the religion of great Cathedrals and African villages, were casual worshippers at home. An octagonal closet near the State Apartments had served as a chapel until, in 1843, Victoria's new ballroom swept it away. Her architect, Edward Blore, conceived the idea of relocating it in one of a pair of unsuccessful conservatories on the West Front (the other became a swimming pool). The conservatory Chapel Royal lasted until 1940, when it became the only room in the Palace to be destroyed by a German bomb.

A few years later, when Britannia came to the throne, she built a new chapel on the same site . . . almost. In post-war Britain, a gesture to democracy was always desirable, especially when the only inconvenience was to the church. The new Chapel Royal was smaller than the old, having to share its site with an art gallery, where the paying public could see selected Royal treasures. None the less, Britannia had re-established a home for religion, and contributed to the Palace's ramshackle evolution. A benefactor's pride augmented for her the cosy pleasure of family worship in the Chapel, and such a pleasure, known regularly over many years, inevitably fostered deep faith.

She had not lost it when her life fell to pieces. A polite God could not be expected to intervene. He waited discreetly in the Chapel Royal for her to make a visit, ushered her in among the velvet and gold, commiserated with her that the family was absent again, and smiled on her devotions, understanding that, of course, she did not come to anticipate His paradise, but to remember her own.

Major-General-Lieutenant-Colonel Omar Gutz, of American Euroforce High Command, was lunching at John Wayne's. He put the leg of a chicken into his mouth and revolved it slowly with his tongue, sucking and gnawing at the white thigh. His fat fingers drummed idly on the table. He was waiting for the young man sitting opposite to organize his words.

'You see, sir, the English *are* happy to have us here. But we've found that it's best to keep some of our operations . . . low key. I particularly feel that to requisition these farms in Kent would . . .'

He looked up at Gutz's uncomprehending pig face. The chicken bone stuck an inch out of his mouth, his right cheek bulged with its fleshy end, the facial muscles worked in a disgusting ritual of mastication.

'Would *what*, Major?' Gutz removed the chicken leg with a pop and put it on his plate. Shreds of white flesh ran in spittle down its sides.

'Major Garbo.' Gutz leaned across the table. 'Just remember that we do not *have* to consult the British government about anything. This island is part of a military operations zone. We can do what we like in Kent or anywhere else. We are preparing for war here!'

'Yes sir,' said Garbo calmly. 'But my job . . .'

'Your job is to be nice to the Prime Minister. I know that, son, and we certainly want his co-operation. But what we want more is housing for our missiles while we're waiting to position them in France. The existing depots aren't full yet, but after the new year we'll be building more. You've got until then to make the British understand why we want those farms. If you don't, we'll take 'em anyway.'

Garbo nodded. Of course they would take them anyway. But if diplomacy broke down, he would be held to blame. And he liked his job. He liked living in London.

'O.K. sir, now just let me get this clear. You won't build these new depots in Kent so long as there is storage space available within say . . . what area?'

'Oh, maybe, seventy-five miles from the coast. But you can't just shove a Zee 10 warhead in some old cowshed, boy. Those babies need space, security, a stable temperature.'

'I know that sir, but I'll give it some thought, if you don't mind, before I speak to the P.M.'

'You do that Major, and get back to me. Always glad to help you liaison boys.' He picked up the sodden chicken leg and engulfed it in his face, still talking, but no longer intelligible.

They came out of the restaurant into Soho Square. A staff car was waiting for them. Ten minutes later, they had moved round the corner and were stuck in traffic on Charing Cross Road. Gutz began to curse.

'Goddamn, Major. These streets must've been made for horses! I've got to get to the Ath'neeum Club by two. Meeting an old buddy of mine for lunch.'

It was Garbo's job to keep important people happy. He told the driver to try a detour, and the big car nosed along Denmark Street, St Giles church ahead: a pile of discoloured stone with a warty spire and a paralysed clock.

'Jesus Christ!' said Gutz. 'Is that a church?'

'There are hundreds like that in London.'

'What a dump! Can't we give 'em some money for new ones?'

'Not worth it, sir.' Garbo nibbled at a ragged fingernail. 'No one uses 'em anyway.'

Then, after they had passed the church, he turned suddenly to look at it again.

While the warm weather lasted, Edward and Christina regularly spent their afternoons in the Blue Suite. The danger of being caught by the Queen added excitement. There were signs that she too was a frequent visitor.

Once she left her reading glasses on the mantelpiece in the Sitting Room. Every minute of that afternoon was charged with the expectation of her return. And on another occasion, a month after she first besieged them there, she left out her book. Edward came from the bedroom to collect his cigarettes, and found it on the floor by the chaise longue. Did Britannia really lie on that thing? He shuddered at a memory of Christina.

'Good God! Guess what the old girl's reading?' He carried the book back to bed. Christina took it from him and flipped to the title page.

'Sir Robert Filmer. Who's he?'

'A Restoration apologist for Divine Right.'

She stared at a page of the crabbed, heavy print, put the book down and yawned. 'I know the sort of thing. All touch-pieces, and charts tracing the Royal Family back to Adam.'

'Touch-pieces!' Edward exclaimed. 'That's what those coins in the study are called!'

'She's really gone off her rocker if she believes in all that,' said Christina.

He lit their cigarettes. 'Divine Right was once a very potent concept. There are shreds of it even in our present constitution. You'd be amazed how much power Britannia still has, in theory.'

'She has nothing!' Christina scratched her thigh.

'Well, you needn't sound so triumphant about it!' He was startled by his own indignation. 'Isn't it enough for you that she's losing her marbles? I suppose she's got you rattling the door handle and backing out of the room?'

'Yes!' Christina laughed. 'And Bracken too. The Witch is furious. Perhaps this book is a clue to it all. Bracken also has an explanation.'

'Tell me.'

'George Three and Charlotte were crazy about protocol – rattling door handles before entering, not sitting down in the Royal presence, not turning your back . . . Hardly surprising if Britannia is going the same way, it's all in the family. According to Bracken, they ended up too dignified to eat. They had a meal laid out every night, and just sat there with their eyes averted, not touching it!'

Edward picked up Britannia's book and noticed that she had turned down the corner of one of its pages. He opened it and read aloud.

'"We muft keep the King's Commandment, and not fay: What doft thou? BECAUSE WHERE THE WORD OF A KING IS, THERE IS POWER, AND ALL THAT HE PLEASETH, HE WILL DO!"'

'But you know, Chris, it couldn't have been worse than the system we've got now.'

November. A day borrowed from freezing January, and the Queen, wrapped warm for the State Coach, leaves Buckingham Palace to perform her only remaining public duty; the televised Opening of Parliament.

In spite of the cold, and a bone-cracking ride in the eighteenth-century coach (a pantomime vision, made real by order of a mad king), in spite of having to see the detested men of government, and to pronounce their policies in her own name, she enjoyed the adventure, the attention, the chance to put on a Hartnell frock (how they had lasted!), and of course, the chance to adorn herself with jewels. To see the world from under a diamond tiara was, she had long understood, unfailingly to see it as a kinder place.

For the ceremony at Westminster she would wear her proper Crown again – so loaded with jewels that the neck could hardly bear it – and she would sit on her actual throne. Would this be the last time? Would the State Opening be obsolete by next year?

Not if one were to judge by the splendour of the occasion. She almost believed in it. Her Cinderella coach was drawn by eight gorgeous bays. Who was to know they had not come from the Palace Mews? The Master of the Horse rode behind in his own fine equipage, and was followed by five more State landaus. What television spectator could see through their darkened windows, and discover that they were empty?

How little her people knew of her condition! How could the cheering crowd in the Mall know that these soldiers of the Household Cavalry who escorted her coach were really film extras, hired for the day, dressed by Berman and Nathan's? Perhaps, if they found out, if the millions watching at home found out, there would be a national outcry. Surely the British people would not tolerate such an insult to their Queen.

The helmeted horseman immediately behind the State Coach tugged at his ill-fitting chinstrap until it broke, then spoke to the rider at his side.

'How much do we get on top for riding these bloody horses then?'

'It must be a one-er. Especially with this weather. They got a bloody cheek making us work in weather like this. I shouldn't be surprised if it snowed. No, I won't take less than a one-er for this.'

'I turned down an easy day on the new Bond film to do this,' said the State Coachman to his companion. He looked over his shoulder. 'Harry's in the Cavalry this year. I wonder how much he'll get on top.'

They were standing in a giant gilded scallop which formed the Coach's footboard. The Coachman's assistant chipped off some paint with the toe of his boot and looked at his watch.

'Should be off by two, though. It's an easy gig really. You been on it before?'

'Yeah. Every year since '95.' They passed under Admiralty Arch. The spectators lining the route through Trafalgar Square roared their appreciation of the spectacle. 'Course, in them days there were real crowds,' said the Coachman. 'The English still came then. This lot's just foreigners. French, Italian, Spanish. Keep the bloody game going they do.'

His assistant looked over the waving jolly crowd. Sleek bodies, good teeth, bright nylon jackets. It was true; there was not an English face among them. Any fool could see that.

Britannia waved gaily from between the two palm trees that framed the coach's window. It was such a pity she could not stop and talk to the people. But she retired into the padded interior when passing the Banqueting House in Whitehall. She was afraid to look at the place where her ancestor had been executed. Yes, they had gone that far once.

In the past Tony had always been there beside her in the Coach, to comfort her at any unhappy moment. But he was dead now, and she was being driven alone to Parliament.

She was roused by cheering boys, her traditional welcome from the pupils of Westminster school – the sons of American families stationed in Europe. She was puzzled by a banner they were holding up. At last she decided that a word was missing; surely something should come after BRITANNIA SAYS RUSSIA SUCKS? Even so, it would be a peculiar and, as far as she could remember, an inaccurate claim. Why were Americans forever putting words in other peoples' mouths?

Then came the arrival at the Palace of Westminster, the greeting outside the Lords by those two old bit-part players, the Lord Chamberlain and the Earl Marshal. They walked backwards as they led her to the Robing Room. She was always glad to see the tension on their faces as they struggled to keep in step. So long as the Government paid even lip-service to Royal tradition, she would have opportunities to prove that superiority of manner was no mere act.

But in the Robing Room, she blanched at the prospect of spending hours under the Imperial Crown; what more was it to her now than a heavy reproach? And she hated this public act of cooperation with the members of her Government – the nosepicking column-jugglers and calculator-jockeys of the Commons, who in any case saw her presence as a nuisance, an interruption to their endless bickering. Nor was the Lords any bastion of civilized politics. For twenty years, no senior minister had left the Government. One by one, their names had been submitted to her for elevation to the peerage. She had sanctioned each title with the taste of vomit in her mouth.

It was an aristocracy of foaming union-bashers and New Company string-pullers – the white-haired architects of penny-pinching Britain, earthly representatives of Norman St Margaret, founder and martyr of their sect, who had died after refusing to pay for his own heart-transplant.

So, after the dressers had finished with her in the Robing Room, after the progress through the Royal Gallery, the background-action pages, yeomen, ladies-in-waiting, gentlemen-at-arms (with axes and plumes – all props, all extras), after the Panto Queen had been enthroned in the Lords and Black Rod had done his turn, here came the Kitchen Sink Government.

Tadpole led the way, Britain's charismatic Prime Minister. Britannia never saw him without a guilty sense of relief that he had discontinued their regular private meetings. She could not in any case, have answered for his safety at Buckingham Palace. He belonged to that order of life which, these days, ran the risk of being cooked and eaten by the few remaining members of her staff.

Then there was Tadpole's young American advisor, the mysterious Major Garbo. His prominence here was as incorrect as it was unmistakable, and Britannia saw the television cameras shy away from him. Would they find anyone half so photogenic among the handful of Opposition members, now creeping into their places for the ceremony?

No, they would focus on her in the end, on the after-all unquenchable dignity, the star quality of her state. She was ready for her close-up now, ready to introduce the real plot, the latest diabolical attempt.

The Lord Chancellor came forward with the Gracious Speech. She noticed that his heavy robe made him smell. He was the man who had once talked her into the Britannia Box commercial. All smiles then, he sneered at her now; the kind of courtier who carried poison in a signet ring or a wristwatch.

'Try not to take too long, ma'am.' He curled up his mouth at her. 'We'd like to finish debating the Workhouse Bill today.'

She pretended not to have heard him and glanced at the bold-typed first sentence. 'This year, my Government' . . . How that possessive pronoun hurt!

But it was time to begin, to carry on regardless, to let her talent shine through this appalling script. The house was silent. The titled ladies – those New Company wives – popped lozenges into their mouths and thought about Harrods while, under the lights and the beady cameras, Queen Britannia spoke.

'This year, my government . . .' The print seemed to lose its definition. She could not read it. She stopped speaking. In her vanity, she had forgotten to put on her glasses. She fumbled with a cloth-of-gold handbag. But before she had opened it, she knew that the glasses were not inside.

Someone shouted 'Cut!' And the Lord Chancellor came panting over to her. 'What's the matter?' he asked curtly.

'My glasses,' said Britannia, staring hopelessly into her empty bag, 'I seem to have left them at home.'

'You stupid woman!' he hissed. Britannia looked at him in astonishment. He shrugged and muttered, 'Oh well, it doesn't matter.'

A member of the television crew came up and said, 'Are we going on?'

'No,' said the Chancellor, 'announce a technical problem. Transmission terminated.' He stumped off to speak to Tadpole, pulling off his robe as he walked.

Britannia remained on her throne, suddenly tired, blinded by tears. Nobody took any notice of her, except for the television man, who hovered uncertainly in front of the dais, then climbed up, and with his back to her, addressed the room.

'O.K. everyone, that's a wrap. You can go home now. Thank you.'

After the disaster at Parliament, Britannia took to her bed in a fit of depression. She knew that her public career was over. They would never let her out of the Palace again. Bracken was with her constantly, and Christina did not interfere. The Witch's administrations would either drive the patient from her bed, or kill her.

One morning, while Bracken was attending the Queen in her bedroom, Christina listened at the door. She was curious to know what happened in the hours the two old women were alone together. At first it was only Britannia's voice, struggling to recite some strange-sounding words.

'Nam . . .Myo . . .Ho . . .Ren . . . Oh, Bibi,' she whined, 'it's so very difficult!'

'Myoho Renge Kyo,' Bracken supplied, in a firm monotone.

'Ho Renge Kyo . . . Are you *sure* it's necessary, Bibi?'

'It is ancient wisdom,' said Bracken. 'If you had chanted all your life, you wouldn't be in such a mess now.'

'Is it all just retribution?' said the Queen plaintively. 'I never thought . . .'

'It is Karma. Perhaps you were bad in a former existence.'

'I haven't been bad in this life, have I, Bibi?'

'You have been complacent.'

'Oh, but it's been such a strange life! First it seemed I could do no wrong. Now everyone is absolutely beastly. Surely the next life will be nicer.'

'You must chant,' Bracken admonished, 'or you might come back as a slug.'

'A *slug*?' Britannia wailed.

'Yes. Or a stone.'

'Not even as a horse, Bibi, not even as a corgi?'

'Not unless you chant. Now, let's do it properly. Kneel before the Butsodan and contemplate the mandala. Before you begin to chant you must ring the bell seven times.'

Christina heard seven thin chimes, then Bracken and Britannia's voices joined in prayer.

'Nam Myo Ho Renge Kyo . . . Oh no, I can't!' The Queen broke off. She was becoming peevish.

'You must,' Bracken ordered. 'Morning and night!'

'No!' Britannia's voice was childish, imperious. 'I shan't chant, ever. Now leave me.' There was a rustling sound as Bracken gathered up her dress. 'And take away this silly cupboard!'

'It is the Butsodan, shrine of the sacred mandala.' Bracken spoke with quiet menace. 'And you would do well to respect it, my girl!'

'Leave me,' Britannia repeated.

Shortly afterwards, from a window high in the South Wing, Old Malcolm watched Lady Bracken hurrying across the Quadrangle, with an elaborately carved wooden box under her arm. 'Aye,' he growled into his beard. 'She's the one, the Devil. Her Majesty'll nae convaert till that midden's gone tae her heathen hell!'

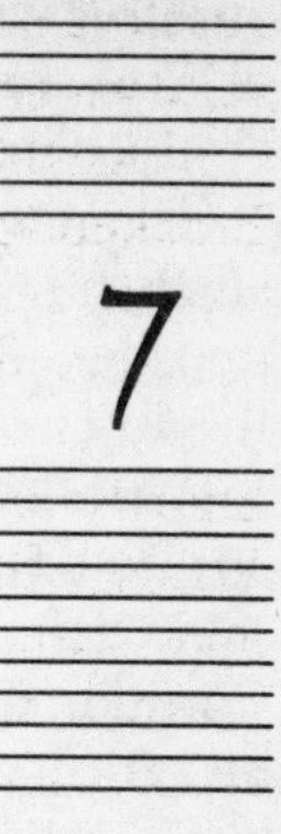

In December, Palace life became very uncomfortable. Summer had been too generous, there would be early snow to balance the books. None of the rooms were heated; their occupants made use of the old fireplaces. Wooden furniture began to disappear from the corridors. There was electricity for the East Front and the North Wing, but in the south Old Malcolm lived his pious life by candlelight.

Vane stood at his bedroom window one afternoon, staring glumly across the spiny landscape of St James's Park. The charmless, metallic winter had always been there, it seemed, and always would be. There was no consolation in the sight of the tourists, who even in this weather, waited hopefully at the Gate, in case Britannia should appear. He could not share their optimism. He turned back to the room. A Louis Seize escritoire crackled in the grate, warming the yellow wallpaper. But there was no consolation, no solution. He sat down. He gnawed his lip. He was obsessed.

He needed to earn a quarter of a million pounds, very quickly. The cocaine/plasma trade was finished;

an American-backed coup had toppled the Government of Chipoquaqua. And Erika had only half the money to pay for her son's operation.

He picked up his book and started to read. If he made an effort, he was able to concentrate. After weeks of useless fretting, he was beginning to calm down. Soon he would think of a solution. In the meantime, he read his book.

When he put it down, and as he prepared to go out, he suspected that the answer was at hand.

He left his room and walked along the Chamber Corridor, down the stairs to the Privy Purse Passage, past his office, out of the Garden Entrance, across the grounds and through a door in the Palace wall, to Constitution Hill.

The idea came to him fully as he crossed Green Park. At Green Park station he almost turned back to the Palace; there was something he had to do as soon as possible. But it could wait until morning.

He arrived at Harrow smiling, relieved of the sense of impotence that had dogged him, made him feel like an imposter there lately.

Ian and Erika were putting up Christmas decorations. She stood on a chair in the darkened living-room, muttering at a ragged lighting flex which hung from the ceiling. Ian was underneath, holding a torch for her, hopping with impatience.

'Hold it still, stupid!' said his mother. 'How can I do it? Hold the torch higher!'

'Why don't you get down and let me do it mum? It's so simple!'

Edward stood in the hall doorway. 'I can't imagine what you two are doing, but surely it'd be easier with the lights on.'

'*No*!' Erika shrieked as he reached for the switch. But she did not let go of the naked wire.

Ian laughed. 'He's only joking, mum.'

'Well, now that he's here, he can do it.' She clambered down from the chair. 'Here is a screwdriver. Here is the end of a string of fairy lights. And up there is the wire to which it must be connected, by means of *this*!' She handed Edward an adaptor which had four impossibly tiny and deep-set screws.

'But *I* can do it, mum!' Ian took the adaptor out of Edward's hand and stood confronting his mother.

'He can do it.' Edward assured her. And she took his word for it. She looked at him, saw his confidence, and allowed Ian to climb up on the chair.

Edward handed over the screwdriver and the string of lights, then stood back. Erika held the torch now; in its dramatizing light, she looked like a painting of an anxious supplicant. Her face was getting thinner. Worry was changing her physically. But it would be all right. It would be all right.

'How is it, darling?' Ian had been working silently for five minutes. Erika saw him rubbing his nose. 'It's not too hard for you is it?'

'I'm nearly there,' he said quickly. And in a minute he jumped down. Erika shone the torch in his face.

'Don't do that!' he snapped. 'It's ready.' He ran over to the light switch. Edward took Erika's arm and pulled her toward the wall so that she could see the full effect of the decoration.

'Da da!' Ian filled the room with festival light. Edward watched the flush of pleasure on the woman's face, then glanced at the boy.

A second later he felt the body next to him stiffen, and he knew that she had seen it too. Ian's nose and upper lip were smeared with blood. He squeezed her hand.

'It'll be all right, Erika. Trust me.'

As soon as he got back to his room the next morning, Edward picked up the book he had been reading the previous day, and took it downstairs to the Blue Sitting Room. He left it on top of the bookcase. If the cold was not keeping Britannia away, she would be sure to find it.

Macrobe slept on his back, the blanket pulled up selfishly to his chin. He slept soundly. Next to him, Peter Pounce opened his eyes and looked down at the canal. The traffic on the bridges was bumper to bumper. Weak sunlight pinked the roofs of the Waitings, the grass along the banks was still frosty. Without looking at his clock he knew what time it was.

He propped himself on one elbow and contemplated the sleeper. Under the bedclothes his hand circled slowly up Macrobe's thigh towards the groin. But he stopped short, gave an experimental squeeze, then pinched hard with his thumb and forefinger. Macrobe squirmed, kicked out, tried to wriggle away, but Pounce caught him with both hands and pulled him back. The boy settled against him, still snuffling for sleep. They lay together for a minute. Then Pounce leaned down and whispered, 'You'll miss breakfast.'

Immediately Macrobe abandoned cover and swung his feet to the floor. He rubbed his arms to fight off the first fit of shivering, then stood up and began drunkenly, silently to dress.

Pounce watched closely for boys' idiosyncrasies in this universal routine of dressing. Two feet might be thrust into one trouser-leg or the head into a hole made for an arm. Socks were usually inside-out, laces seldom attended to, hair never. He had watched hundreds of boys dress on cold mornings, a sequence of them running back through his life to the archetype: himself, or his image of himself, as a boy. He was more than twice Macrobe's age, but he remembered how it had felt to be fifteen more clearly than he remembered last week.

The way boys lurched into their day – that desperate carelessness – was the essence of it; the stupid suffering expressed on their faces. They saw themselves as dreamers, tyrannised by an incomprehensible adult system, based on cold mornings. They lived in frustration; it amounted sometimes to madness, often to violence, and was remembered later in life as the first, the strongest, and the most heroic passion.

Pounce worshipped the memory of it, steeped himself in it through the boys he slept with, and watched it come out in the silly way they dressed in the mornings.

'I want you and Microbe to work at the Golden Age again today,' he said when Macrobe had sufficiently constructed himself. The boy nodded and stumbled off to breakfast. Pounce lay back and stared at the ceiling.

He needed a new project for his workers. A major source of cocaine had failed, and supplies were running out. There was no immediate financial problem, but the boys had to be kept busy. They would continue to work the arcades, but that did not offer the same sense of achievement as drug-pushing. If he had not lost Damon, perhaps they would be ready now to start rebuilding the dome . . .

Damon. He had been gone for more than three months, but Pounce wanted him too much to give up on him. There was always a chance that if he went down to Kings Cross this morning, he would find him there.

A German tourist was pumping pound coins into a fruit machine, unaware of their value. He lost all the money in his pockets, and went away smiling to change some more. Macrobe took his place. He gambled a pound and collected ten. Peter Pounce stood a few feet away, keeping a lookout for staff.

'I think there may be more to come from that one, Mac,' he said. 'Try another coin.'

He watched the boy induce a secondary spill, then realized that his other charge had gone out of sight. Microbe had been marking a punter further down the arcade, but evidently something had distracted him. Calling Macrobe to assist him, Pounce searched among the banks of machines for some minutes before spotting the younger boy in a remote corner, holding a fifty-pound note in his hand. He was staring at it in disbelief. Then he pocketed it and smiled up at the man who had just given it to him. It was Miss Gunsmoke who smiled back.

Pounce retreated behind a machine and waited for Macrobe to come up.

'Your brother is over by the wall, talking to a policeman.' Macrobe looked frightened. Pounce took out a fifty-pound note and handed it to him. 'It's O.K., just give this to the cop, take Microbe's arm, and walk him away. There won't be any trouble.'

He waited out of sight until red-faced Microbe was brought up to him. 'You boys start for home,' he said, 'I'll catch you up.'

Miss Gunsmoke came round the corner at speed a few seconds later, looking worried, and walked straight into Peter Pounce. Pounce glazed over, smiled as if at something else, and stepped out of the way. The cowboy hunched his shoulders and fled. His enemy stared after him, swallowing a torrent of unseemly faggot abuse that had risen suddenly in his throat. One day, he would put that bastard down for good.

*

On a black midnight, some weeks before the birth of Christ, Old Malcolm came up from the South Wing, to the sitting-room of the Lady-in-Waiting. No light showed within. As he had guessed, Bracken was still with the Queen. He opened the door and slipped inside.

Monstrous shadows loomed in front of him, spectral shapes, filling the room. He gasped and staggered back, groping frantically for the light switch. He got a hold of himself; it was only the effect of light from the street. But when he found the switch and the shadows were banished, they left only a naked horror. Old Malcolm crossed himself.

'Aye, 'tis the devil's lair, right enoo,' he whispered.

The detail of Evil was overwhelming. He gaped, and tried to make sense of it, starting with the chamber's gigantic centrepiece, a low-hanging chandelier in the shape of a lotus flower. Its light was diffused through green petals to the lower half of the room, and flung upwards on to foliage encrusting the chain; glistening enamel leaves, climbing to the crimson ceiling, disappearing into the mouth of a . . . Old Malcolm looked away, to corners where seductive landscapes glimmered in black lacquer, to chairs supported by leaping fish, to candelabra that were snakes and self-devouring dragons. Dragons leered at him from the tops of cabinets and clocks, writhed at the feet of gowned sages, lurked by switches and handles, stalked long-legged birds in the wrought gold frames of mirrors. The birds waded out along the top of the wainscot, into a turquoise river; above them, fruit trees grew into a yellow sky. In the trees, canaries sang. Could he hear them? When he turned away, did they hop from branch to branch?

He fought off the devilish distractions: the winged snakes that flew up from the carpet, the bowls of bright metal flowers, the laughing buddhas, the bells, the fringes and tassels blurring every edge, the unfathomable polished surfaces, the patterns seen through patterns on every object, everywhere he looked. He would not be deflected; he fought through to the red-marble table between the windows. The table's furniture was not strange in this room, but he knew by its arrangement that this was the significant site, the evil heart, the altar.

There was an incense burner with a filigree top; the Shantung curtains were fragrant from its smoke. There was water in a porcelain dish and a bowl of fresh fruit. There was a bronze buddha, a jade figure, and a bell, but Old Malcolm did not disturb these things. He bent down and plucked the little cupboard from the back of the table.

He carried it into the middle of the room, feeling its knotty ornamentation under his fingers. Then he stopped, set it down on the floor, and opened it. A chart was pinned to its back wall; a mysterious diagram, minutely annotated. Otherwise the cupboard was empty, except for the top of a matchbox which was pinned to the inside of one of the doors. It was a souvenir packet, of the kind sold to tourists, and showed a picture of the Queen's head.

'Sweet Jesu!' He stood up too quickly, slow to regain balance. When he wiped his brow he noticed that his hand was shaking. How much time was left? At that moment a clock chimed in the room, a jewel-eyed dragon snapped its tail. There was no time.

He defied the Devil, scooped up the cupboard and ran wildly with it to the door. But listening, panting before the last dash, there was the slap of Bracken's slippers outside in the Chamber Corridor. He had just time to switch off the light and retreat with his prize behind a tall lacquer cabinet. Then the door opened, and her pointed shadow fell across the room.

He heard a slight jangling of bracelets as she entered and shut herself in. Then she moved out through the green lotus-light, to a pier glass opposite his hiding place, and started to dismantle her pagoda of hair.

It had changed colour lately, the natural white was dyed black, and those supporting skewers, once wood, were ivory now. Everything about her was more dramatic; she had let her Oriental obsession come fully to the surface. He knew why. Her winter gowns were richly coloured and threaded with gold. The jewellery was pendulous, hypnotic. And those much-travelled slippers were not scuffed as before, but embroidered and bright black; another damning sign of self-appointed priesthood.

She was reaching up to remove the second kanzashi from her hair when she saw him in the mirror.

'You, Scotsman!' She turned fiercely. 'What are you doing here?'

Her eyes settled on the box he was hugging to his chest – those evil eyes, extended in dark makeup on to her cheeks, the long flat lips that were painted to match.

He stepped out of his corner, defied her without speaking.

The Witch remained calm. She advanced on him slowly with one arm outstretched.

'Give me the sacred Butsodan.'

She spoke with authority, trying to unnerve him, but he held his ground.

'Ye'll nae be gaen abroad wi' yer cupboard agin', My Lady! 'Tis nae concaern o' mine wha Devil waership ye pratise here. But ye'll nae be waerkin' yer evil on Her Majesty. Nae while I'm alive tae stop ye.'

'Barbarian!' Bracken flared out. 'Jacobite! What can you know of these mysteries? Squeezer of bladders! Give back the Butsodan!'

'Nae, woman! 'Tis for yer aen soul as well as the Queen's, tha' I'll burn this box taenight!'

'Burn?' She grew taller, glowering in the green light. '*Burn*!' She rushed at him and clamped his arms with her fingers; he could feel long nails biting through his clothes. He was frightened; her face floated in front of him, malicious and mocking.

'Devil!' He spat at her.

Bracken reeled. Her lips parted in a snarl. She started to shake him violently. He was helpless; she would shake out his strength, his sanity, his soul. The tower of her hair bobbed angrily above him. If he could loosen it over her eyes, he might gain advantage from her disorientation. He dared to hold the box with one hand and with the other snatched out one of the lower kanzashi. A long hank of hair fell and waved in front of her face, making her look madder than ever. But it was not enough to distract her from the fight. She was taking advantage of his weakened hold on the box. She had it in her long fingers and was wrenching at it with supernatural strength, grunting through bared teeth. He knew she had won. In a minute she would have the box, and him, in her power. Then he remembered the kanzashi in his free hand.

He slashed at her with it, making a long stripe on her cheek. She howled and her sharp fingers swiped at him, but he dodged and struck again with the hairpin, using it not as a claw this time, but a dagger. He raised it high in the air. The bayonets spared no one on Culloden Moor. He drove the kanzashi into her neck.

For a long time he sat on the floor, next to the corpse of the Lady-in-Waiting, wondering what to do with it.

There was a lot of blood; it had spread across her Chinese rug, forming a dark halo for Bracken's head. He decided to roll her up; the rug was not large. And as he worked, slowly, painfully, he had the idea of dragging the body to the lake.

It was a journey of more than a quarter of a mile from the top of the East Front to the lake at the end of the garden. But he had all night to make it. For a quarter of an hour he tugged the long bundle northwards past the empty suites of the Chamber Corridor. But when he reached the occupied section, he heaved Lady Bracken on to his back, in case the noise of dragging her should wake the sleepers. He knew that the Secretary to the Secretary seldom slept in his room. But he had seen the Corridor's other resident, the foul-mouthed girl, coming and going at all hours.

He paused by her door and listened. Once in a while she brought back a fancy-man, and there was moaning and groaning to be heard. Tonight there was only his own heavy breathing, and he staggered on under his burden, muttering, 'Och, well, she's a midden a' the same.'

He kept the bundle on his back till he reached the North-East stairs. He meant to roll it down in one piece, but somehow the end of the rug became trapped under his foot, and when he launched it, Bracken bounced out and bumped away on her own to the landing. Malcom stumbled after her, then sat down to rest on the bottom step, too tired to repackage her straight away.

She lay in the moonlight on the marble floor. One eye stared balefully out, the other was lost in the wreckage of her hair. He needed a long rest, but could not bear to sit looking at her. He fetched the rug and wrapped her up again, talking to her as he touched her, in order to keep down his fear.

'Wha' a way tae make yer last jaerney thrae the Palace, eh, ma high and mighty lady? Come then noo lassie, over ye go, 'n dinnae make a soond by Her Maj'stey's door, the poor thing needs her rest.'

He had to drag the body along the King's Corridor; he was too weak now to carry it. And once he had safely passed her bedroom, it occurred to him that Britannia might be drugged at night. On the strength of that possibility, he took Bracken by lift to the Garden Entrance. His fear of waking the Queen was not as pressing as the need to conserve his own energy.

He was fighting exhaustion. He had been travelling for an hour, bent double in hot exertion, or shivering with cold and fright. And worse was to come outside.

Outside the cold was militant, windborne. The grass in the garden, calf-high and spiky with frost, cut his hands. It kept sliding him back on the gentle incline of the West lawn. Twenty minutes after leaving the Palace, he had advanced less than a hundred feet. After thirty minutes he began to pray. His work no longer warmed him; the cold was affecting his muscles. He prayed for his old muscles, shouting the words to keep himself upright. And when his prayers began to sound like questions in the empty night, he sang a Highland song.

He came over the hill singing. The lake was spread before him in the moonlight. 'Wa hey, My Lady, we're haem!' he cried. And they skimmed over the grass to the shore.

But it was not the right place to dump her. He had already decided on the bridge. Having got this far, he could not leave her bobbing about in reeds at the shallow edge. The bridge went out to an ornamental island; from it she would go straight into deep water. But the bridge was on the far side of the lake.

The temptation to compromise strengthened him.

There were many places along the shore which might have been suitable, and every one passed-up imposed further glorious torments of cold and fatigue, with the added slimy martyrdom of lakeside mud. But the bridge was always that much closer, and after half an hour, he became certain that he would make it.

In fact he was reaching out for the first post of the railings when he slipped. He had slipped a dozen times on the bank, but this time, tears came into his eyes, and he very nearly cursed his God. What had he done to deserve this misfortune, to get so far, at such a cost, to get so close to his goal, and then to sprain his ankle?

He lay in the mud, scarcely more alive than the woman at his side. This was where they must part company. He to crawl, God willing, back to the Palace, she to find her own way to the bottom of the lake. There was still a chance of it, if he gave her a good push; the bank was steep here and vegetation sparse.

Wincing from the pain in his ankle, he got to his knees and hauled Bracken into place between himself and the water. The effort he put into shoving her off unbalanced him; he saw only that she was gathering momentum before his face hit the mud. There followed a period of oblivion.

He understood one thing clearly; the loathsome bundle was still half out of the water. The weight of the upper part had slewed it around until it could not roll. He wriggled down the bank and put his arms round Bracken's swaddled reluctant legs.

He meant to pull her out a little way and straighten her, but as soon as he had a good hold, she lurched and dived, dragging him with her into the lake.

The first contact with the freezing water paralysed his muscles, locking him in an upside-down embrace with his victim. Above their heads the moonlit bridge wobbled and disappeared. Then somehow they slipped the sheath of the Chinese rug, and floated away together.

The snow came to London that night. By dawn the Palace stood in a Russian landscape, and a sheet of thick ice covered the lake.

8

For many weeks, Britannia did not leave her suite in the North Wing. Meals arrived as usual – so far they had not tried to stop her meals. Bracken came daily, nightly. The girl physician came when summoned. The secretary was not summoned.

Then Bracken stopped coming. Outside, the world turned white, noiseless. An unprecedented silence: there was no bagpipe music at breakfast. She sent to enquire the reason, but no answer came, and she forgot.

To keep warm, she burned the dining-room chairs, even the one Tony had sat in. She could not let herself save it, that would be madness, and madness would be defeat. Next, she burned her desk, but continued to sit in her chair in the bay window, staring out for hours at the white, unchanging world, waiting to be included in the petrification of nature, the numbness. Life had surely finished with her. But it would not let her go.

She took refuge in sleep, in whole days of unconsciousness. But there were times when she was awake, and acutely unhappy. She thought she would go mad if she did not speak to someone. Her only visitors were the footmen who brought her food, and to talk to them would be madness in itself. She missed the stern guidance of her Lady-in-Waiting, even the wretched Butsodan. She planned an expedition to the South Wing, to find Old Malcolm and hear him talk about the Catholic Stuarts. She planned to pray again among the Anglican ghosts in the family chapel.

But for many weeks, she did nothing.

One day she left the Palace altogether. The weather had not let up. From her window, the ground looked hardly negotiable. But she decided, after lunch, to go for a walk.

She put on stout clothing – her Balmoral kit for 1989. How marvellous to be in walking shoes again! She felt energetic; she clomped down to the Garden Entrance instead of taking the lift. Then she was out in the stinging air and walking briskly up the drive. At first, the ice underfoot was a little frightening, but she was in her stride by the time she reached the Forecourt.

There, she felt the first thrill of being out in the world again. Above her was the Palace her people knew; Aston Webb's bluff facade, the Balcony, the boxed soldiers. Did visitors wonder why the Guard never changed now, why it was always just those two toy soldiers staring out, stock still from their little huts on either side of the Grand Arch?

Today, there were no visitors waiting by the railings. Surprising; she had thought they could be relied upon in any weather.

But perhaps it was better to avoid close contact with the people. She might have forgotten herself, and begged them to help her.

St James's Park was also mysteriously deserted. It was so like being in the country again. She felt she could walk for miles, and had only one regret: no corgis to watch rummaging in the snow, to whistle to, to talk to. The Government had taken them away.

She crossed the park diagonally to the top of Birdcage Walk, then hurried along Storey's Gate, to the Broad Sanctuary. Without stopping, she entered Dean's Yard, the green quadrangle of Westminster Abbey.

The Recognition
Then the Archbishop shall say:

> Sirs, I here present unto you Queen --------, your undoubted Queen: Wherefore all you who are come this day to do your homage and service, Are you willing to do the same?

The people signify their willingness and joy, by loud and repeated acclamations, all with one voice crying out,

GOD SAVE QUEEN ---------.

Then the trumpets shall sound.

No schooling could adequately have prepared her for it; a young English Queen coming to be crowned. Already, at twenty-seven, she was a veteran of tedious solemnities. The Coronation was a long-distance event; she practised with sceptre, sword and orb, learned the meaning of the Wedge of Gold and the Ruby Cross, the Ring, the Rod and the Glove . . . All part of the family game, all remote from her now.

She stood in front of the altar, where the throne had been placed on that day . . . it must be nearly fifty years ago!

What she would never forget was the thing she had

been least prepared for; the noise of the crowd. In the past it had been her father they cheered for, or her mother, or uncle. But there had been no escaping the fact that on the day of her Coronation, she was the star occupant of the State Coach. They were cheering for her, and louder than ever.

There had been no escaping it. Yes, that was how she had felt about it: slightly frightened. On that day she became public property, even friends and family looked at her as if she was going off on a long sea voyage. Of course they were all enjoying the game, getting dressed up and riding in coaches, being splendid for the new television cameras. And the Archbishop was such a dear, giving her that impish, reassuring look as he presented to her the Sword of State:

> With this Sword do justice, stop the growth
> of iniquity, protect the holy church of God,
> help and defend widows and orphans, restore
> the things that are gone to decay, punish
> and reform what is amiss.

Of course. Naturally.

But all the time, the great church was being buffeted by the cheering from outside. It pressed against the stained glass windows, gathered in the recesses of the roof and rained on her; the voices of children, women and men, massed and distilled, heard by their rulers as a ghostly baying.

After that, things got back to normal. Of course there was a well-established formula for meeting the wishes of the people. They spoke to the Monarch through their elected representatives. One simply had to follow the advice of Governments.

In that case it was the will of the people that she should die poor, powerless and lonely. No, she did not believe that. It was a mistake. Somehow the constitutional mechanism had broken down.

She stood very still and listened to the silence around her. The Abbey hoarded its dignity like a ruin, simply endured, by strength and beauty. It at least was indifferent to its own uselessness.

She tilted her head back and stared at the vaulted roof. A ray of weak sunlight travelled from a high clerestory window, dappling the top of a pillar with coloured shapes. The vision was transitory and uplifting and Britannia, ready for God's consoling effects, strained her senses towards Him.

But He had nothing to show or say to her. No explanation of her life's misfortunes boomed out of the architectonic heaven. No fatherly Voice dismissed her in peace. There was just a persistent echo of the past; the massed voices of her subjects calling to her, reproaching her.

'Oy! You! What d'you think you're doing?'

A man had appeared at the far end of the church, by the Great West Door. He came bustling down the nave, and when he was close enough, she guessed that he was some kind of caretaker: a stocky, bearded person in a donkey-jacket and a peaked cap.

'Excuse me madam, I'm talking to you!'

She stepped down from the altar platform and met him on the flagstones.

'Don't you know the Abbey is closed today?' He smelled strongly of spirits and his cheeks were flushed.

'But where are the clergy?' Britannia asked.

'At home, I expect, madam.' The man seemed slightly taken aback. 'They wouldn't be here, would they? Not on Christmas Day!'

'Christmas?'

'Not that they're here even when it ain't Christmas,' he confided, suddenly switching his mood. She could see that he was very drunk. 'I don't see anybody for weeks at a time now.'

'I didn't know it was Christmas!' Britannia was agonized, wringing her hands.

'Sometimes, ma'am, it gets so lonely here, I could take comfort in the bottle.'

'Oh, my People!' Britannia fell to her knees in front of the caretaker, and pressed her face into his jeans. 'Oh, I have let you down!' she sobbed. 'I have deserved my misfortune.'

He brought up a fat hand and patted her gingerly on the shoulder.

'Now then, girl. It can't be as bad as all that. Why don't you come on and have a nice cuppa?'

9

Her ancestor, George Two, had considered St James's Park too good for his people. He consulted Robert Walpole about the possibility of turning it into a private pleasure garden for the use of the Royal Household.

'How much would it cost, d'ye think?'

'Only a crown sir,' said the minister.

That autocratic fatuity had cooled slowly in the Blood; a legacy of Divine Right – the preposterous doctrine of Royal infallibility. Yes, it was preposterous; she admitted that. A fraudulent social contract. But even cranks like Filmer had one strong argument in its favour: it had worked. For a long time, it had been good for England.

What had replaced it? Two hundred years of rule-by-parliament had reduced the monarch to a human being, another hundred to a beggar. That was how it was for the Queen. And the people, in whose name these things were done, how was it for them?

Better to suffer under an ostentatious tyrant than a committee of clerks. Better to be kicked than tricked; better a torturer than an advertising man.

She was standing at the window of the Blue Sitting Room, looking across to the park. After the Abbey she could not go back to her suite in the North Wing; *these* would be her rooms had she been allowed the choice. But the touch of satinwood would not soothe her today. There was a new excitement which was not discharged through her fingers when she wound the Cupid Clock. She gazed out of the window, clutching a slim volume she had found on top of the bookcase.

She had never seen it before, but its author was familiar: Lord Bolingbroke, a rambunctious eighteenth-century statesman, exiled by the Whigs for his Conservatism, exhumed a century later by Disraeli who hailed him as the father of the Party. For both men, to be a Conservative was fundamentally to respect the throne. How far they were from the party which used that name today, from Norman St Margaret and his snivelling successor!

Britannia sat down in her reading-chair and opened the book. *On the Idea of a Patriot King* was Bolingbroke's title. Yes, that was a nice idea. It had a nice sound to it. But what did it mean?

So, the author catches his reader. So, Vane catches his Queen.

And finds himself, one January morning, rattling the study door; summoned for the first time in months.

He found the room changed. Most personally significant was the absence of any chair for him to use during the interview. But far more notable was the fact that Britannia's desk had vanished, particularly as she herself seemed unaware of it. She sat in her usual chair, with the garden behind her, watching him advance. He positioned himself by guesswork, the breadth of a desk away from her, and inclined his head.

'Good morning, ma'am.'

Her smile was gracious. Certainly she behaved as though the polished surface still separated them, the avenue of framed photographs. She sat straight and businesslike, and in her lap, as if it were out of his sight, she was holding his copy of Bolingbroke.

'Good morning, Mr Vane. I trust you have had a pleasant holiday.'

'Very pleasant, thank you, ma'am.' In fact, Ian was sick. He had taken to his bed on Christmas day, and the outlook was bad; he was losing ground.

'Well now.' Britannia was slightly breathless, as if uncertain how to begin. Her hidden fingers fretted along the edge of the book. Vane moved in sympathy, from one foot to the other, wishing she would get on with it, or offer him a seat. After a minute, still shy, the Queen went on. 'As usual, Mr Vane, it is to seek your advice that I have asked you here. I wonder . . . that is, I want to help . . . to be . . . useful . . .'

'Ma'am?'

She looked straight at him. 'To the country.'

'But ma'am,' he smiled soapily, 'your services to the electronics industry have been . . .'

She made an impatient gesture. 'That was a mistake. Do not condescend to me, Mr Vane.' A flash of authority; those eyes he couldn't meet. Oh yes, she was ripe for him.

'For the sake of the Britannia Box,' she said quietly, 'I have sacrificed my integrity, my impartiality. Agree with me that that is the case.'

He shifted his weight, cleared his throat, looked at the ceiling, then let her have it. 'Yes ma'am, it is the case.'

'Yes.' She looked down, understanding that the horrors must be catalogued, faced fully. 'Used! Tricked by my own Government. Trivialized. Brought into their scheme . . .' her grey head began alarmingly to wobble, 'into their pettifogging scheme of things.' The pitch and volume were rising, the tone incredulous. 'And do you know what they are trying to do, by cutting off my money, taking away my staff, publicly insulting me? They are trying to tell me that I am . . . am . . .'

He supplied it. 'Redundant, ma'am.'

Unspeakable. This was the crisis. She was very still and quiet. He could have comforted any other woman, put his arm around her to ease any ordinary pain. But let Britannia suffer! This would be her spring of anger, boosting whimsy into a practical plan; the rattled handles and petty sadism (how long would he have to stand there?) into a political force. He waited. The silence stretched, became a strain, became his shouted silent instruction to her: 'In your hands! The answer is in your hands!' How long before she remembered? The drooping grey head, the wandering mind. Was he wasting his time? Was she even awake?

Then she turned over the book in her lap, glanced at him. He smiled, drawing her out. And tentatively, almost inaudibly, they began.

'But the country . . . my people. Will they accept it? Have they truly lost their respect for me?'

He didn't hesitate. 'No ma'am, they have not.'

'Aaah . . .' She took a minute to follow an encouraging thought, and stood up suddenly. 'I have been reading . . .' She came out from behind the desk, walking around it into the room and held out the book with a long, steady arm. 'Take it, would you Mr Vane. I seem to have lost my glasses. The page is marked, I think. I'd like to hear the passage underlined.'

He took the book and read aloud, '"The cause of the people he is to govern, and his own cause, would be made the same by their common enemies."'

The Queen's face came into focus, nodding agreement. 'That is the Patriot King. Whose heart is truly with the people. How easy it is to be distracted from them, either by too much power . . . or too little . . .'

Something about her face now, was new; more than the reflected light of Bolingbroke's rhetoric. Ah yes, that was it. What healthier sign of defiance in women than the sagging skin staunched with powder? She turned away from him and wandered down the room.

'You see, we have suffered together, my people and I. Like me, the poor lost their state subsidies when the New Companies came. Like me, they have been either ignored or bullied into silence . . .'

She was dressed more smartly too. Those lime-green pleats had not been seen a dozen times since the New Zealand tour of '86.

What unimaginable coercion had imposed on the Queen her taste in clothes?

'Do you have a coin, Mr Vane?' He located a pound in his trouser pocket, but she did not come for it. 'Of course you have one! Every Englishman carries an image of me: my claim to defend the things he holds sacred. Fidei Defensor: Defender of the Faith . . .' She stopped, and he saw her shoulders working, the white face puffed up with laughter. 'I didn't even know it was Christmas!'

Back at his end of the room now, her attention went suddenly out through the window. She stood by her phantom desk, slack-mouthed; nobody home. He was taking a risk with her; she could become unmanageable at any time. He remembered the open book in his hands and recalled her in his best bedside voice.

'"The cause of the people he is to govern, and his own cause, would be made the same by their common enemies."'

'Their common enemies!' Britannia breathed the words deeply, reviving. Then she was in again, at the deep end. 'This makes me think that I should have the support of the people . . . were I to act . . . against the Government.'

At last! He had to show a little surprise, but rushed in immediately, before she had a chance to falter.

'The people ma'am . . . are waiting at the Palace gates, for you come out and lead them.'

'Yes!' She was with him all the way. Her eyes sucked in his confidence, then she hurried round the desk and sat down, talking business.

'Of course, I have retained certain powers . . . The Government thinks I'd never dream of vetoing a law, or an appointment, but aah . . .' She trailed off, the head bobbing with bloody revenge.

'You *do* have the powers ma'am,' he said calmly, 'but they are a little rusty . . . To be plain: how would you exercise your Prerogative, when convention has placed it in the hands of your enemies!'

'I should simply deny them the use of it!' Britannia trumpeted. 'I should use it against them. I should dismiss them. Then, I should hope for a spontaneous demonstration of popular support . . . You have made me believe that I should get it, Mr Vane.'

'Ye-es,' he conceded. 'But if you were to do something unexpected, something no monarch has done for hundreds of years; if you were to interfere with Parliament, the initial response would be one of shock.' He paused. She was listening like a child. 'That would give the Government an advantage. They would dismiss your revolt as an aberration, a misunderstanding. And the people would believe them . . . They would think you had gone mad . . .'

He heard her gasp. Fear of that disgrace would keep her with him, watching his shaping, weaving gestures as he paced in front of the desk.

'But you could count on popular support if you called for it *before* taking action. If you went directly to the people, and formed an alliance with them, the Government would be simply squeezed out . . . swept away.'

Britannia clapped her hands. 'We could have a revolution!'

'There's no need for that ma'am,' Edward smiled. 'Englishmen can still voice their opposition through the ballot-box. Of course no one believes that they will; the people with jobs think of nothing else, the unemployed are drunk or watching television . . . and everyone expects to die in an American war. The Government feels safe. Elections have become a rubber stamp. But while the machinery of democracy exists, it is a weapon for your cause!'

'Mr Vane, how wonderful!'

'A political party could be established in your name, just as an electronics company was. It would be a monarchist party, a true Conservative Party, with a policy to restore you to real power. If we work hard, we can transform the nation before the next general election. We'll have a landslide victory!'

His arm swept down, drawing down pictures from heaven. Britannia wriggled and bit her lip. 'Go on!'

'As soon as it took office, the new government would resign – as promised in its election manifesto – and all power would revert to you. You would be free to choose your own ministers and advisors, and always to act according to your own sense of what is best for the people.' He bent towards her. She gazed rapturously across the desk. 'You'll be able to do what you like, ma'am.'

'Oh, Mr Vane. I want that!'

He straightened. The book was in his hand and he turned to the last page.

'"What spectacle,"' he declaimed, '"can be presented to the mind so rare, so nearly divine, as a king possessed of absolute power, neither usurped by fraud, nor maintained by force, but the genuine effect of esteem, of confidence, and affection; the free gift of liberty, who finds her greatest security in this power, and would desire no other, if the prince on the throne could be, what his people do wish him to be, immortal?"'

'Oh, but Teddy, it's all so hideously old-fashioned.'

'Is it?' Edward cocked his head. For the first time Christina had shocked him with a display of wilful ignorance. Talking Britannia round had drafted expedient self-belief to his effort. Great wodges of history were patched into the argument. He walked painfully across his office to the Italian chair, a restoring whisky in his hand.

'I see it as prophecy. Lord B. had black visions: a good people exploited. Corrupt Parliament unchecked by cringing royals. How he longed for the Faery Dyke herself to come sailing up the river! Or any crazed Stuart would do. He was certain that the Germans would ruin us by pussy-footing with politicians. Three hundred years later, it turns out he was right.'

He kicked off his shoes, drank some whisky, lectured the garden through the glass wall. 'And why did it take so long? An economic accident. Prosperity blurred the issue. Parliament behaved itself during the Empire. The Crown was allowed a semblance of power; a sort of special effect for savages, both domestic and foreign. Victoria did very nicely out of that . . . Everything was very polite until the money ran out . . . right up until the nineteen-nineties. Then Parliament decides that everyone is worth only what he can earn, or swindle. And our Queen takes her true place among us: a Swiss maid on a yoghurt pot, the tart on the bonnet of a sportscar, the scourge of stained underwear . . . I'm not boring you, am I Chris?'

'A little. What are you going to call your party?'

'The Patriot Party . . . Ah God, I'm in agony! She must have kept me standing there for an hour. Why don't you come and massage my shoulders?'

'I'm trying to fix a lash. If you didn't inflame Britannia's ridiculous autocratic fantasies, she might drop all this protocol.'

'Ah, but it's worth it. Besides, she might have burnt the visitors' chair in order to keep warm.'

Christina was operating on her face; trying to salvage last night's makeup with a compact-mirror, under the light from his desk lamp. 'I'm still not sure that it's worth it. You haven't explained why you're taking all this trouble.'

'Why do I do anything these days?'

'For Erika.' She snapped shut the compact and poured herself a Scotch, then came over and sat on the floor by his chair, resting against him. 'You realize that this will finish Britannia off, or at least drive her completely mad.'

'I don't see why. Things will be small-scale at first. There's a by-election for Islington South in a few weeks' time, to replace that M.P. who choked to death at the Ball. I think the Patriot Party might make a nice debut in that constituency. It incorporates the Waitings.'

Christina turned and looked up into his face. 'It is all for Erika though, isn't it?'

He shifted on the chair and winced. 'Oh please give my shoulders a little rub, Chris.'

He stood near tinted windows in a handsome, high-up office. Between flat columns of natural brick, a floor-to-ceiling scene of Victorian rooftops, stacked with uneasy snow in the first sun of the year. He sipped a cup of coffee. The office overlooked a gloomy canyon, yellow-striped where sunlight broke through between the buildings. Some gulls dived past, were briefly gilded, then settled on the surface of the canal.

'Is it O.K.?' said the boy who had brought his drink.

'Fine.' Edward smiled, but the boy went out without looking at him. A minute later Peter Pounce arrived.

'Sorry I wasn't here to meet you, Edward. Had to get one of the boys off to hospital.' He held out his hand. 'Just a check-up. Can't be too careful. Leukaemia; I've lost some good lads.'

They sat casually, on opposite sides of a low glass table. Pounce poured himself coffee and Edward, who had asked for the meeting, felt obliged to talk.

'I've always liked this office. Did you design it?'

'One of the boys did. Fletcher. He was here a couple of years ago. Very talented.'

'Has he continued in this work?'

Pounce shrugged. 'Who knows?' He drank a mouthful of coffee. 'Fletcher lost his looks. They all do.' He put down his cup. 'So. What's up? A new source of supply? A new stimulant to sell to the sotted rich?'

'No, I'm thinking more of a stimulant for the poor.'

'But the poor can't pay enough,' Pounce grinned. 'And besides, it would be wrong.'

'Not necessarily. It seems to me that your boys must be underemployed just now. I have some work for them. As you say, there's no money in it. But you would have the satisfaction of seeing the Government seriously embarrassed.'

Pounce looked out over the rooftops of the Waitings. 'Now *that* would be a stimulant for the poor. I'm interested.'

Ninety minutes of fast talking with Peter Pounce had secured a team of reliable election workers. As he walked back to Kings Cross Vane started to think about his next job: finding the candidate.

It was nearly lunchtime. Smells of warmed-up offal oozed from the warehouses into the filthy streets of the Waitings. People with nothing to eat sat on the steps for scraps that would come their way later. Those beyond food, with nothing to wait for, hunkered down with a bottle, or the toxic lung of a polythene bag.

A large number of women had formed a queue by the entrance to a wood and canvas lean-to. Inside, a big round-faced man was tending several makeshift ovens, humouring dogs and children drawn by the smell of baking bread. Edward watched him put a batch of loaves into a basket made of fencing wire and carry it to a trestle table set up in the mouth of his den.

'Now then, Mrs Strichen,' he said to the first woman in the queue. 'Can you pay me a pound piece today? Oh, that's lovely.' He handed over two loaves. 'Well, and how are we today, Mother Blasedale?' The accent was Welsh. 'A little better for the weather I'm sure. That's it, no no, a fifty will do. Pay me when you can. And you, Mrs Singupta; one or two today? Oh don't you worry about that. We'll see how we go.'

When the ovens were empty, and the baker had finished his business, Edward approached. Evidently his presence had already been noted; the Welshman beamed a sceptical welcome across his table. 'Now then, sir. You've not come to tell me the great ones of Whitehall have agreed to hear my case.'

'No,' said Vane, 'not exactly . . . Perhaps we could go inside.'

'I don't see why not. I'm ready for a cup of tea now. I hope you'll have one too.'

The bakery was built in a former loading yard; the

cobblestone floor was scrupulously swept. It was little more than a canopy around the chimneys of the ovens, with stacked bags of flour serving as walls, chairs, even as a bed. The ovens themselves were massive, made with recycled bricks.

When the baker had ushered his guest inside, he brought in the table from the doorway, and pulled down a canvas flap. In his cosy privacy, he became even more genial.

'Albert Bridge is my name. My father gave it to me after taking a bet in our village pub. It has made me a sober man, and slow to take offence.' He set a kettle on a hob built into one of the ovens, then stood up, wiping floury fingers on his apron. But he did not hold out his hand. 'Now as I think of it, you'll probably know my name already, if you're from the Government.'

Edward stressed his innocence. To settle the issue, he sat on the dusty top of a flour sack, mortifying his dark suit. Albert Bridge seemed satisfied, and ready to wait for the guest to explain himself.

While they drank their tea, Edward looked at the sacks piled ten deep on every side, enclosing the baker's life.

'You keep a large stock of flour, Albert. Do you buy it locally?'

Albert shook his head. 'It's from my own store, in Peterborough. I was a baker there, you know. I left this flour behind when I could no longer afford to use it. I came to London to complain. But when I realized how long I'd have to wait, I decided to make bread for the people here. It took the last of my money to have the sacks sent down by train to Kings Cross. But I earned it back after a while; there's even a few pennies to send home now. And the work keeps me busy; I'm luckier than most.'

'But you weren't from Peterborough,' Edward probed, 'not originally.'

'Oh no.' The Welshman's face hardened. 'I only came to the flat country to find work. And I found it. That's what makes me so bloody angry, you see. I was doing all right. But I might as well have stayed in my lovely hills.'

This was beautiful. This was perfect.

'It must have been hard to leave the place you loved,' said Vane.

Albert Bridge nodded solemnly. He poured them both another cup of tea, and began to tell his story.

The Queen's handkerchief was old and very worn. Really, there was nothing left of it but a border of nineteenth-century Nottingham lace. She found a corner that was not already sodden, and dabbed her eyes. It was so sad, the life of Albert Bridge.

The Secretary to the Secretary had brought her a leaflet prepared for the Islington campaign. One side was printed with a biography of the candidate, the story of a prosperous provincial baker who had tried to remain in business for himself. When the New Companies were formed, he did not invest, though he could have come to profitable terms with the Bakery New Company, which needed a Peterborough base for its stock brand, Mother White's.

Albert Bridge had preferred to stay with his life's work. In the early 1980s, he had been the last apprentice to the ancient firm of Milksop and Crabbe, whose bread had been known in every Edwardian household by the legend on its wrapper, 'Strong And Brown As A Darky's Arm.' As the century wore on, sales declined steadily until, at the time of Albert's apprenticeship, this delicious bread was unknown outside farmhouses in the remoter Fens. Nobody before him, it seemed, had connected the bread's marketing problem with its old-fashioned wrapper. And like any ambitious young man, he kept quiet about what he knew, until he could be the one to profit by it.

That time had come when the last Milksop died, and the assets of the bakery were to be sold. Albert went to his bank manager with a scheme for rescuing the firm, and within a year he had moved it back into the national market with a slogan for modern breakfast tables: 'Grit your teeth with Bridge's Bread.' Then the Bread New Company had come along.

He was no match for Mother White's promotion and distribution. The growth rate of his market slowed. He made a late application for shares in the new economy, and was sold one of the notorious 'dormant' companies. Ten years later, he had seen no return. Meanwhile, his sales figures began to drop. Loyal employees, whose jobs he had once confidently guaranteed, became a liability. Soon he could not afford to keep them. Soon he could not afford to keep his own family . . .

There was also a photograph of Albert Bridge on the leaflet. He was standing outside his bakery in the Waitings, arms folded across his chest, thin hair slicked straight back, a shiny-faced paragon of muscular philanthropy. Oh yes, Britannia thought, the Patriot Party can rely on him.

But could it rely on her? On the reverse of the leaflet was her own picture. She confronted it with dismay, a sense of misgiving. She was shown as a much younger woman: a tinted, postcard image from the 1960s. Robed, statuesque, dark curls rippling around her tiara. In those days she could at least have brought young strength to a conflict with the Government. But that was a quality she no longer possessed, any more than she possessed her former name.

Ten years ago she had signed a document. Her name

was no longer her own. She was to be known only as Britannia for as long as the Electronics New Company needed her. But the Patriot Party did not recognize that agreement, and the postcard portrait reclaimed her as the namesake of England's most famous, most feared female ruler.

The manufacturers of the Britannia Box would certainly be very angry to discover that she had sanctioned this leaflet. Her Electronics Company pension would be immediately suspended. And what would the Government have to say about this slogan: DIGNITY FOR MONARCHY, and this pledge: We will restore to our Queen the majesty of true government, the personal rule of a Royal Patriot.

They would finish her off for good this time. They would move her to a bungalow in Cheam, and fill her palace with clerks. Who would stop them? Could she really expect her People to save her when they realized that she was not the noble girl of their picture, but ragged, wretched and seventy-seven?

It was hard to maintain a belief in the vitality of the People, shut up in this exclusive ruin. Their voice could not be heard here, or even remembered.

Fewer members of the public had visited the Palace in her reign than in any other. Oh, she had tried . . . those gruelling garden parties of the middle years! But it had always been such a circus, such a fenced-in, officially-routed rodeo! These corridors and galleries, where Victorians of no particular importance had wandered at their leisure, were known to her own people only through the slaverings of columnists and hacks.

It all came down to the media. Modest accessibility had been sacrificed for a worthless mass appeal. She had let them do it: 'It's the modern way, ma'am . . . too many of them for any *real* contact . . . You leave the People to us . . .'

So how could they see her as part of their life, their suffering – winter heating bills and the inadequacy of pensions? Surely the Government could rest easy. No amount of Patriot Party propaganda would establish her as a popular heroine.

But only a few weeks ago, the silence and grandeur of the Abbey had swept away those years of media babble, and she had remembered how the voice of the people had claimed her on the day of her Coronation. In the Abbey she had understood that weakness and misgiving were forbidden her. And that the claims of the people endure, though Kings and Queens ignore them for fifty years, for a hundred or a thousand.

Two Parisian students who had come to see the Palace were sleeping rough in St James's Park. At dawn the girl woke and peeped out of their lair in the shrubbery. She saw an old woman walking along the lakeside path. The girl wriggled forward in her sleeping-bag to get a better look. An English quality was here in essence; unmistakable and awesome to French eyes.

They took in its detail: the coat – too long – the flaring skirt and stubby shoes, the hat like a collapsed bucket with a velvet bow, and most of all the colour . . . Could all this be coincidence? When the very model of these brave English ladies lived . . .

The old woman sat on a bench to rub her ankle, then lifted her face in the milder darkness. And the girl saw it clearly.

'Ali! Ali!' She squirmed round and shook her boyfriend. *'Réveille-toi! C'est elle, la Reine. J'en suis sûre. Regarde, Ali! Regarde, le* Limegreen!'

The boy muttered and fumbled with his glasses. He examined the old woman for a minute then turned sharply aside.

'Oh, tu te trompes, Nicole! Elle est vagabonde. Elle est folle. Tu peux bien voir. Elle se parle toute seule!'

She is talking to herself. This is a new development. And where is she off to, unable to sleep, with so much to think about now, plans to make, after so many wasted years? There aren't many places to go dressed like that. She is off to church.

The change in the sky was half complete when she arrived under the western towers. This second trip had been harder; she had stopped to rest in the park. But she came to the Abbey like a bride returning, to confirm herself in a girl's half-understood vows. Love and duty. In the Abbey she could believe it was not too late.

The archway to Dean's Yard was deep and still obscure. She did not see the barricade across its middle, and walked into barbed wire, hurting her hand. A thin dark line appeared on her palm, running up to the tip of the forefinger. Advancing again slowly, she allowed her eyes to get used to the dark, and saw that the archway was blocked.

But there were other ways to get in and out of the church, learned during a hundred security briefings for state occasions. She made a long detour around the Abbey precincts, and came up Little College Street to Westminster School. From an alley next to one of the boarding houses she got into the Abbey Garden. Then by a slimy and unpromising sequence of passages to the Great Cloister; she had remembered a door at the side of the nave through which the choir entered for services.

A sweet relief to slip in through that door to safety. Then sudden disorientation, a physical shock of air displaced, pushing her against the wall.

The whole of the nave was occupied by a snouted rocket, rising at an angle from the west, past the pillars of the north aisle to the level of the arcade, forty feet above the floor. The space, the balance, the sweeping perpendicularity of the church, were reduced to factors of support and accommodation; it had been turned into a garage.

Britannia advanced a little way towards the monstrous tenant. Its cylindrical flank curved away to catch the light settling in from the high windows of the nave. She was crying, shaking her head, mumbling denials of the visual evidence.

'No, no. It can't be. They would never . . .' She went closer, and stretched out an arm. Her forefinger touched the metal. Withdrawing quickly, she denied the evidence of touch. 'It can't be.'

The snout, high up, held itself against the light, gaining definition as the east windows took colour. Britannia turned abruptly and fixed her eyes on the door.

'It is not there.'

She walked across the flagstones without looking back.

'It is not there!'

But where she had touched it, the missile was smeared with her blood.

10

On a bright February lunchtime, ten boys marched up and down outside the gas showroom in Upper Street. Islington shoppers hurried by, smiling, familiar with the daily spectacle. The boys were dressed as little soldiers. There were six fifers, in short red jackets, gold-braided in front, with blue cuffs and collars. Behind them marched four drummer boys, whose jackets were blue, with red facings. They all wore white cross-belts with a short sword; their trousers and spats were dark blue, boots and peaked shakos shiny black. The tune they were playing, *The British Grenadiers*, competed shrilly with the traffic. Two other uniformed boys, not in the band, handed out leaflets to members of the public, and politely refused any offers of money.

The show ended promptly at two o'clock, when the midday crowds had gone. The boys dispersed to canvass the residential areas, the streets of squatted warehouses, those council estates that were still habitable, those that weren't, and the renovated Georgian enclaves of middle-class liberalism.

Watcher worked along an exclusive street near the Angel. There was someone else going from door to door, about ten houses ahead of him. Once, while he stood at the top of some steps after knocking at a door, he saw the other person accost a pedestrian. He remembered what it was like to beg in streets like this. Then the door opened behind him and he was invited inside. He took off his shako and entered. When he came out, the beggar was waiting for him at the gate. The boy who had run away.

'I recognized your ginger mop when you took your hat off.'

He wasn't such a tough customer now that he was hungry, Watcher saw. 'You won't get much round here. Better off up West.'

'I just need a quid to get started on the machines.'

'What machines?'

'Golden Age, of course.'

'That's our territ'ry.' Watcher started to walk towards the next house. 'You try your luck up West.'

'Come on mate,' the other boy followed him. 'Give us a quid for a cup o' tea.'

'Peter don't let us carry money around.' Watcher turned to face him. 'But he'll take you back if you want. He's O.K. like that.'

Damon didn't reply, but tagged along while Watcher made his next call. They climbed the steps to the front door, but it opened before they reached it and a woman appeared. She looked straight over their heads at the sky. 'Rain later!' She rudely examined the visitors. 'Yes. What is it?'

Watcher thrust out the leaflet with Albert Bridge's picture.

'Her Maj'sty the Queen commends a friend of liber'y, madam.'

The woman took it and read quickly, critically. 'The Patriot Party. Yes, I've heard about it, but I'm in rather a hurry just now I . . .' She was holding the leaflet out for Watcher to take it back, and saw his face clearly for the first time. Immediately she withdrew her arm and stepped aside in the doorway, smiling. 'Well, I suppose I could spare a few minutes. Why don't you come in boys, and have a piece of cake?'

Damon was hardly aware that Watcher had hesitated. He pushed forward at the mention of food, and allowed himself to be hustled into a sitting-room at the back of the ground floor. Watcher followed, but remained standing, with his shako under his arm, while the woman made tea in an adjoining kitchen.

He stationed himself by a dirty glass door, which opened on to a yard. It looked as though the yard had not been swept for years; paper and rotting leaves were piled up in every corner. The brick walls had once been painted white, and the creeper on a smashed trellis had been alive. Under the trellis was a neat row of empty wine bottles. There was also a tiny flower-bed containing some skeletal sticks and, near the door, a mouldy plastic dish, for a cat which had long since deserted.

'I've seen you before,' the woman called out from the kitchen. 'The soldier boy. I think I've seen you at Kings Cross.'

Watcher did not answer. He was standing next to a varnished table, marked by hot mugs and cigarette burns. Like every other surface in the room, it was loaded with books, mostly paperbacks. He noticed the title on one fat spine: *For Their Own Good: How to Help Others Against their Will.* He picked the book up and showed it to Damon.

'What d'you reckon that means?'

Damon shrugged and shook his head.

Watcher noticed another book. It was open and face down; evidently the woman was still reading it. The title was obscured by a packet of cigarettes, but some words on the back cover puzzled him: *Why do Adults Abuse Teenagers*? But did they? As far as he knew, it was usually the other way round. Before he had a chance to investigate more closely, the woman came in from the kitchen, with two mugs of tea.

'There's no cake I'm afraid. My husband must've taken it to work; they've just closed down his canteen. He's at the Arts Council.' She handed Watcher his tea. 'Yes, it *is* you I've seen at Kings Cross. How could I forget that hair? It's almost the same colour as my son's.' She turned away and picked up her cigarettes. 'He died when he was fourteen – of leukaemia. I blame the Government; they should never have allowed the Americans to bring their missiles here . . . so many accidents.' She sat down in a rotting, old-fashioned armchair, and lit a cigarette. 'But of course, your Patriot Party would send the Americans packing. Am I right?'

'Oh yes Madam,' Watcher launched into his patter. The woman sat quietly for a minute, then interrupted him.

'You are from the Old Brewery, aren't you?' She looked at Damon. 'Both of you?'

Damon nodded.

'Her Maj'sty is resolved that all American bases . . .' Watcher recited.

'And you actually live there?'

He looked at the woman. 'Yes missus.'

'And that man . . . What's his name?'

Watcher was all innocent incomprehension suddenly, silently stonewalling. She turned to Damon.

'He looks after homeless boys, doesn't he dear?'

Damon waited for Watcher to help him, but Watcher had withdrawn from the conversation, and was staring out at the yard, drinking his tea.

The woman smiled encouragingly at Damon. 'Were

you homeless, dear? I'm sorry, I don't know your name.'

He told her.

'It's a shame that such lovely, handsome boys should . . . Where do you come from Damon?'

He told her.

'Oh, that's a lovely part of the country!' She sucked her cigarette. 'We've some friends up there. They live in a mill. It must be quite near you. And how old are you, dear?'

'Scuse me missus.' Watcher turned round and held out his empty mug. 'D'you think I could have some more tea?'

'Certainly, dear.' She stood up, leaving her cigarette in an ashtray on the arm of the chair. 'I don't suppose either of you can be a day over fifteen.' She went into the next room.

Damon opened his mouth to reply, but this time Watcher glared at him to shut him up. 'Come on,' he whispered, 'while she's out in the kitchen. We're going.'

Before they left, Watcher put his boot on the seat of the chair and pressed down. In the cavity that appeared between the cushion and the arm, a quantity of straw stuffing had accumulated. He picked up the burning cigarette and dropped it on top, then removed his weight, letting the cushion spring back into place.

They ran up the street to the Angel, and on to Pentonville Rise. Kings Cross was spread below them, walled by the spired hulk of St Pancras Station. Watcher squinted at the clock tower.

'Three-fifteen,' he said. 'We'll be back in time for tea.'

11

Alexander Tadpole, Prime Minister of Great Britain, Americanisation-apologist, earthly representative of Norman St Margaret, sat in an underlit Downing Street sitting-room, frowning at a letter.

His small mouth opened and closed, but no sound came out; there was no one to hear him, and he was an economical man.

A telephone near his hand started to warble aggressively. He picked it up. 'Yes?' he croaked.

'Major Garbo has arrived sir.'

The door opened before Tadpole could respond, and his American advisor walked in.

'O.K. Alex. Let's have it.'

Tadpole handed over the letter for Garbo to read, removed his glasses and screwed up his face. His moustache tickled his nose. He stroked a vacant scalp.

'Well Max, what d'you think?'

The American, as always, thought too much.

'Seems simple enough to me.' He gave the letter back. 'This guy, Vane, is a businessman. We pay him quarter of a million, and the Patriots don't contest

Islington South. It's a quick way of getting them out of our hair, Alex.'

'But I assure you, they're no threat to us,' said Tadpole. 'This candidate of theirs is little more than a tramp. And the Queen is senile, quite incapable of assuming power, everybody knows that.'

'But why take the chance? Look, I've got a flat near the Angel, I've had leaflets shoved through my door, I see their workers in the streets. Your guy is so sure of success, he's done nothing. And the election is less than two weeks off.' Garbo walked as he spoke, working himself up, beating at Tadpole's complacency with boyish, new-world bluster. 'Alex, I'm worried that this might catch on nationally if they win Islington.'

He sat down where he could see the Prime Minister's face, allowed himself to become calm, then laid it on the line.

'My superiors don't want political instability in Britain. I say we pay this Vane. He's obviously got the Queen under his thumb. I say we pay him and finish it.'

Tadpole looked very unhappy. 'But I really don't see how . . . with things as they are, how I can spare the money.'

'Oh for God's sake, Alex!' Garbo jumped up. 'What's two hundred and fifty grand?'

Tadpole bit his lip and frowned at the floor. 'No,' he announced at last. 'I have the standards of my party to consider. It would be an unthinkable extravagance. And apart from that, Norman St Margaret would never have given in to blackmail. I'm afraid it's out of the question.' He dared to look at the young American. 'And as I have told you all along, it is unnecessary. I give you my word that the Patriot Party will fail.'

'It had better fail, Alex,' said the American.

But he could not leave it there. This was a money-soluble situation, and he had money to spend. When things were costing, things were changing, coming round to the American way. Washington expected him to spend money on the English. That was his job, and he wanted to keep it. He liked living in London.

He had taken his pig superior officer to Lambeth Palace. Gutz forgave the Archbishop for not meeting them at John Wayne's, forgave him for wearing a dress, turning down a job in Disneyland, serving tea instead of Coke. He forgave him because, at the end of the day, the old phoney took their money. They hired every church in London, no questions asked. That was diplomacy.

Garbo found out later that the Archbishop was supporting some nigger terrorists somewhere. But Gutz was happy, he told Washington that he was happy, and Garbo burned in credit till a new price could be set on English cooperation.

All the same, Washington would never condone open disobedience to Tadpole. Vane could not be paid. This election must take place. But someone would sympathize with the American point of view, and accept American gratitude; some civil servant, in an underheated office, lamenting expense accounts and annual awards. Someone would let him sign a cheque.

A different view her great-great-grandmother had from the window of the Blue Sitting Room. Britannia's pink upholstered Mall had been a strip of mud and horse-shit then. But she could easily replace these buzzing clean cars with a slower, living traffic. See the deferential nodding horsy heads as they cantered past the gates! Like a current down the cabman's reins: the sense of Victoria watching.

London was Victoria's imperial city, functioning in her name. But she abandoned it when Albert died, to immure herself at Windsor. How much that said! She could venture into eccentric solitude, sure and certain that it would make her more than ever the centre of attention.

If Britannia had decided to sulk over Tony, could she have bludgeoned the nation into sulking with her? If, like Victoria, she had preserved her husband's rooms as he left them, and filled his bedside glass every night for forty years after he died, wouldn't they have said she was insane? And wouldn't they have been right?

That was how much credit the old smiler had wrung out of the people; English achievers were reorganizing the world then, and the flush of their cheeks reflected on her. When she came back to London for her silver jubilee, she was received as a deity.

This year, 2003, was the fiftieth of Britannia's reign, and everything that had happened in that time had harmed her. Imperceptibly at first, by degrees, with reason. Then quickly, spitefully, with the smack of flesh on flesh. But if a belief in the monarchy could still be discovered in her people, unnourished by sentiment and national success, it would be worth more than all the patriotic ecstasies of self- congratulating Victorians.

For the Jubilee of 1887, platforms were raised to the rooftops of Piccadilly, and the Queen was driven between waving walls of hands, hats, flags, carpet-bags, aspidistras, bibles and umbrellas. When that crowd cheered, elephants died all over Africa. But Britannia only asked her people to wait, quietly, a little longer at the Palace Gate, until she stepped out on the balcony to inaugurate a New Royal Age. Then they would show her a homage no English monarch had ever received.

When the Patriots resigned the authority of Parliament, democracy would have put into her hands a power that had eluded the most energetic tyrants. It would make up for everything done in democracy's name to her and her kind. And it would happen soon. Soon.

She walked away from the window, out into the Sitting Room where Cupid and Father Time struggled on through unmarked hours. The pedestal clock had stopped weeks ago, shortly after her last visit. And though she wound it whenever she came, she could not set its delicate hands. She could not have said, had there been anyone to ask her, whether it was early in the morning now, or nearly night.

She searched uselessly in satinwood drawers for the key to the clock. Surely she had left it in the commode . . . All this would change; on the first day of the new regime a Clockwinder would be appointed. Time would be precious then; she was old, and there was a lot to be done.

The search for the key brought her to the dwarf bookcase. She remembered why she had come to the Blue Suite today, and sought out a voluminous memoir of the Elizabethan court. She took it at once to her chair by the window. That glorious past; she hunched over it, devoured it. The present could not compete.

Minutes, or hours later, she was disturbed by a noise from the next room, the Blue Bedroom. She crept and put her ear to the interconnecting door. Was there a slight creak, a whisper? Had somebody moaned or sighed? No. Sometimes she worried about herself, suspected that the empty Palace drove her to invention. Soon it would be filled with busy people.

She started to walk away. What had she been doing when she heard the noise? She stopped, turned, went briskly back to the door and threw it open.

But although she searched meticulously, under the bed and behind the curtains, as well as inside a large wardrobe of yellowy burr elm, she found nothing, no one.

Erika did not eat him any more. Anthropophagy was out. She had lost her appetite, and did not eat him, all night, like German sausage squeezed between her fingers. They lay side by side, a counsellor's married couple. Neither slept; she listened in case Ian should need urgent medication, or help getting to the bathroom. He racked his brains for another way, a last chance to save the boy, and himself.

Peter Pounce suspected that his favourite was keeping out of his way. He went looking for him one evening, a few days after Damon came back to the brewery. He tried the common room first; no luck. Some of the boys were polishing boots, or whitening their cross-belts with pipeclay. A group at the table was building a scale model of Buckingham Palace. That had been Pounce's idea; he had hoped it would interest his architect, bring him more into the community. But Damon remained aloof. Cooperative, hard-working even, but mistrustful. Pounce asked if anyone had seen him. Macrobe said he had lent him his squash-gear; he was downstairs in the gym.

He played vigorously, punishing the little ball. Ah Damon . . . Peter Pounce watched, unseen, from the doorway.

As usual, Miss Gunsmoke's influence had been disastrous. What kind of person could treat a boy so callously? He had broken Damon in the bad way, not making him aware, at the same time, of his own worth. It was easy to confirm a child's worst suspicions of adult morality. Damon had been surly before, but pliable, still ignorant. Now he thought he knew the score, the economic truth: never give anything away.

Pounce did not interrupt the game. Damon was beautiful to watch, and forbidding. When he had exhausted himself with thrashing sport there would be a chance to talk of finer disciplines. For now, it looked as though he had a particularly violent resentment to work out of his system.

Pounce stayed in the doorway for half an hour. Then the boy stopped hitting the ball and took off his tee-shirt. Pounce did not want to be caught watching; he could leave while Damon was changing. But he could not leave while Damon was changing . . . He used his tee-shirt to wipe the sweat from his face and body.

Pounce could taste it. Then the shoes came off, then the shorts. Pounce reached for his pocket . . .

But what was that? Those marks on that matchless arse? Two scabby sores . . . but shaped like . . . letters? Yes, it was a pair of initials. Jesus Christ! That was it! Miss Gunsmoke had branded him!

What a sweet imposition, to be treated as a Goddess! She had arrived yesterday, to a trumpet fanfare, at the home of one of her richest subjects. And those had been no ordinary trumpeters, but giants, from out of Arthurian legend indeed! Even before she got in the door, a woman had walked on water for her benefit, claiming to be the Lady of the Lake, charmed to the surface after a thousand years by the beauty of the great English queen, Elizabeth. Then a huge dolphin had swum out from under the bridge, with an orchestra on its back!

The fuss, the feasting, the dancing, the poetry-spouting sprites, leaping out at her from every corner. Such extravagant attention was of course obligatory for a host who desperately wanted her hand in marriage. But oh sometimes, if it had not been her solemn duty to appear amused . . . !

This morning, she had been pleased to find that a hunt was planned; the woods promised simple pleasure, the exercise would be reassuringly human. But now, here was the silly Lord himself, popping out from behind a holly bush, garlanded as a rustic god, all leafy, with red berries in his hair. She had no choice but to slow to walking pace, while he panted along behind her horse (the creature twice fouled his path), extolling her qualities in verse, laying on *her* the responsibility for all these supernatural manifestations, saying that her beauty had set the fairy world a-twitter, that she had enchanted the place, and that were she to leave it, the sun would immediately retire . . .

Oh, the interminable poem, the execrable declamatory style of her noble suitor, the sloppiness of his hack poetaster, who had not even bothered to amend the verse to the circumstances: the sun was not shining in any case; it was raining. At Kenilworth, it was always raining . . .

Britannia knew how Elizabeth had felt. A week at the Earl of Leicester's castle would resemble one of those American tours she herself had made in the old days, before the Americans had lost their sense of fun, or a visit to an endearing but uncomfortable island in the Third World. The hours she had spent sitting on grass mats!

Oh yes, she had been the centre of attention once, but never the centre of life. That had been her downfall. No Bolingbroke could say of her, as he had said of the star of Kenilworth: 'She united the great body of people in her, and their, common interest, she inflamed them with one national spirit.'

But soon she would resemble Elizabeth in every way.

Edward and Christina were in his office, drinking whisky.

'Did you tell the Home Office about Bracken and Old Malcolm?' she asked.

'Eventually. They seemed pleased to save on the salaries. I didn't go into details, I still find it hard to believe.'

Christina made a face. 'Stealing away in the night like young romantics, it's disgusting! Imagine them shacked up together in some Scottish hovel, Malcolm humping her on a sack of oatmeal. Aargh! How can the old and ugly get any pleasure out of sex?'

'It's called love, Christina.'

She looked at him crossly. 'I know that. There's no

need to be sententious about it.' She lit a cigarette to restore her humour. 'Actually, I'm thinking of going in for love myself. Fox-Peeper's just come into some Electronics Company millions, and a house in Kensington Square. He's looking for a wife. I'll have to do something when they finally close this place down and put Britannia in the bin.'

Edward was politely astonished. 'But my dear girl, she is the Queen of Great Britain, soon to be proclaimed the saviour of her people.'

Christina laughed in his face.

By the eighteenth century, the Queen was less of a catch for a nobleman, less the embodiment of national spirit, hardly at all divine. But Anne still touched the sick. They came in their hundreds, every week throughout the reign, offering their repulsive bodies to her fingers, carrying away the talisman, the gold coin which even the poorest kept with them for the rest of their lives.

Britannia was certain now that there were strangers in the Palace. More were arriving daily. At first she had only heard them, coming and going, and only at night. That had worried her. But now that she had started to meet them in the corridors, in broad daylight, it was essential that she got a hold of herself, and accustomed herself to living once again surrounded by people. After all, they were not really strangers. Her first shock of alarm when she saw the young woman on the Ministers' Staircase had quickly given way to a vague warm feeling of recognition. And the girl had curtsied so sweetly, and said, 'Good morning Ma'am,' with such bland self-possession, that Britannia could only respond with a reciprocal dignity. Any other reaction would have been unqueenly, eccentric. She had no doubt that the girl was family, and it followed that the other newcomers to the Palace were also relatives, or friends and admirers, all of whom had come to be with her, to share in the vindication of Royalty.

She made up her mind to hold a State Dinner for her guests on the night of the Islington by-election.

13

Election day. Neil McShane, Returning Officer for Islington South, woke up feeling hot and sick. It was still dark; the day he had dreaded had not even begun. The bedclothes in front of him glimmered mysteriously; he put out his hand, and his fingers touched something shocking. He sat up quickly, switching on his reading lamp. A prodigious fur coat was spread out over the bed. He shook it off, horrified; loose diamonds rolled away and rattled onto the floor. An angel lying next to him turned in her sleep and reached out to him. Recoiling, he got out of bed and phoned her a taxi.

He had never been able to contain either his appetite for pleasure, or his disgust at its expense. He considered himself a truly unlucky man.

Take this girl in his bed. Last night, it had seemed natural that she, an electronics heiress, used to beautiful things, should be given more. Raised for luxury, she adorned it, justified it. She was made to be kept in diamonds and furs, made to be kept in his bed. Now, he would sooner have strangled her than allowed her to sleep on into the hours of his slavery, this frightening day when he must earn the money he had already paid for the hire of her attention.

After breakfast, Britannia walked to the West Front. The State Apartments on the first floor were being prepared for the celebration dinner, but she kept out of the way, only stopping for a moment in the Marble Hall to look out over the Grand Entrance, and listen to a dozen vacuum cleaners sucking the damp and dirt out of the red carpets, bringing them up nicely for the feet of the great men and women who would climb the Grand Staircase tonight, anxious for a glimpse of her.

On the other side of the Marble Hall was the entrance to the Bow Room, with its wide curve of long windows, all open today to flush the Palace with sun and sharp air. She passed through, and on to the Garden Terrace. The snow had gone at last. This morning, she would walk in the grounds.

The lawn was buried in grass. It swept up to meet her at the third step of the terrace, with a comprehensive, portentous rustling. At first, she only dipped her toe in the green uncertain element, testing for a ghost of barbered turf. Then she abandoned herself, and set off into wilderness.

One could no longer see the house from the path by the lake. The long grass added height to the rise in the ground. On this remote side of it, Britannia was effectively diminished, robbed of adult orientation, relocated among the engrossing lakeside phenomena of visits made here, alone and unauthorized, when she had lived at the Palace as a child.

But life could not have been more exciting for her then than it was today. The sunshine in which memory placed her was not warmer than this February sun. Nor had the permanent sun of Victoria's empire been more a symbol of confidence, or the sun self-consciously dappling Elizabeth's path, ordered into the sky by corrupt poets.

She anticipated a revival of court poetry. Understandably, the tradition had withered. There *had* been a man, though . . . Was he still alive? She seemed to remember something about a vole. What she had in mind for the future would be quite different.

She moved rapidly along the lakeside path, singing to herself, smiling, touching the shrubbery with the tips of her fingers. From now on, her presence must touch everything.

Her court must be the centre of cultural, as well as political life. She would not be safe until she was more powerful than television.

This dinner tonight would be the first of many celebrations of her reign. Her reign would be itself a celebration; no truly popular monarch had ever been afraid of pleasure. Every bedroom in the Palace would be in constant occupation. People from all strata of society would be invited to witness the miraculous court. They would go out to foster the legend of its vitality, its accessibility, its taste. Artists would look to it for their first audience. Decent science and stout products would be held in high esteem there. And for the mass of ordinary people, it would set the example of imaginative recreation, of fun.

She walked up on the bridge to the lake island, and stopped in the middle, staring down at the water, remembering that Elizabethan playfulness which had enchanted the moat at Kenilworth. Every Tudor court had had its Master of the Revels, its Lord of Misrule; those wise Kings and Queens had known the value of buffoonery and magic. The belief that responsible people must always be sober was a Puritan heresy, appropriated by the Democrats and served up to young royalty for three hundred years. It got into the Blood, cooled it, coagulated it, kept princes in their places. But now the Blood was up, Britannia was breaking out, and she would have none of it!

This lake setting would be perfect for summer music and folly. Down in the clear water she could easily picture some impossibility, contrived to appear there for her benefit. The more she looked, the more she could see it: the bottom of the lake patterned like a Chinese rug, familiar faces watching her through the water . . . She turned away and continued on to the island. Sometimes the products of her imagination were frighteningly real.

Peter Pounce saw Miss Gunsmoke in the street near Islington Election Headquarters. He was clicking along in his calfskin cowboy boots, coming in the opposite direction, as Pounce was on his way to hear the Returning Officer's announcement. Pounce stepped into a shop to avoid the confrontation, then came out and watched Miss Gunsmoke hurry away to his evening in Kings Cross, letting the full force of his loathing settle on that indifferent retreating back.

He found Vane already on the spot, unshaven, smoking continuously, clearly exhausted, fielding questions from journalists and newsmen.

He was aware of having failed to understand something about his partner's motives. This project, which Vane had introduced as a sort of joke, was evidently important to him now. Over the past few weeks he had slaved for the Patriot Party as if he really thought it could ruin Tadpole, or as if he would rather work like a slave than think at all.

He broke up the press conference and came over to Pounce. 'Did your boys help the old people to the polling stations?'

'All wh

'Good. Do y to vote.'

'We'll know in they're with us?'
the room; a crowded utes.' Pounce looked around
a microphone on a stand. hall, an empty stage with

'He's using a room at the bace's McShane?'
said Vane. 'He had a visitor just collate the returns,'
Tadpole's American advisor, Max Ga fore you arrived.

'Max Garbo,' Pounce repeated.

'D'you know him?' Vane seemed anxious, hunted, tensing up for another dodge. 'I think I'll just . . .' He looked towards a bank of pay-telephones installed at the side of the hall, then fished in his pocket. 'Damn! No change. Peter, have you got a pound coin?'

'Buckingham Palace.' A sleep-slurred switchboard voice. 'Can I help you?'

'This is Edward Vane. Page the Queen's Physician would you?'

'Yes sir, hold the line one moment please.'

He had nothing to hope for except Tadpole's humiliation, and he would fight to secure it. Because of Tadpole, the woman he loved was at this moment watching her son die. She was gaunt and silent now, and he stayed away from Harrow. What comfort could he give? Was it any excuse to say he had tried everything when nothing had worked? His instinct when he picked up the phone had been to dial her number. But he was afraid that Ian might be dead already.

'Chris? It's me. Listen, can you get Fox-Peeper to do you a favour? Can you do it right away? Good girl. I want the dirt on Neil McShane, Returning Officer for Islington South. Sex life, recent bank transactions, you know the sort of thing. Call me back as soon as you can. Here's my number.'

He waited by the phone smoking, tapping his foot.

All these people who had pack[illegible]all to hear the result, what were they hop[illegible] Whose side were they on?

He was on the pho[illegible]ain when McShane made the announcement. P[illegible]ce saw him with the receiver to his ear, listeni[illegible]keeping an eye on the man at the microphone. [illegible]en the tension of the crowd collapsed into noise [illegible]d random movement, and Vane went out of sight.

A minute later, he was crossing the stage, following McShane to his room at the back. And Pounce was pushing forward through the crowd, following too; perhaps even a little ahead.

McShane had his coat on, evidently anxious to leave. But Vane had bailed him up in his office, and was talking rapidly. McShane looked frightened.

Pounce could see them through a glass panel in the door of the office. He tried to enter, but Vane had locked himself in with his victim. The noise from the hall ensured that their conversation, though heated, was private.

McShane was fighting back. He said something which crushed his opponent. Vane stared at him for a moment, then turned away, tight-lipped, and came out of the office.

'It was fixed, wasn't it?' said Pounce.

'Yes, but . . .'

'Was it that American, Max Garbo?'

Pounce's excitement made Vane stop and look at him. He nodded glumly; yes, Garbo had done it. Then Pounce began to speak, and what Vane heard restored him, set him smiling. He took Pounce's arm and walked him out of the building, formulating aloud their new assault.

'They'll all be at Downing Street, celebrating. Meet

me there in two hours, at ten o'clock. Right now, I must go to the Queen.'

In the makeshift election office, Neil McShane hanged himself with his belt from an overhead water pipe. The clatter of the chair as he kicked it over was drowned by the hooting of victorious Conservatives in the hall outside.

For these really grand occasions, the State Dining Room would be inadequate. So a long table, in the shape of a horseshoe, was erected in the largest of the State Apartments, the Ballroom. This meant that the Queen's procession would cover the entire length of the West Front, starting from the Royal Closet, at the top of the Ministers' Staircase.

In the old days, immediate family were rounded up, always there with her; fussing over each others' dress in the last moments of privacy, gossiping, gulping sherry. And of course, Tony's well-worn face smiling, his hand touching hers as the door of the Closet swung open . . .

. . . Having come from the Grand Staircase to the Music Room, the domed and oval apartment at the centre of the West Front, the guests waited for Her Majesty to appear. They hovered around the entrance to the White Drawing Room, glancing in the direction of the Closet, some frankly perplexed, some pretending to understand, others smug and silent. They knew, though it was ten years since the last State Dinner, why there was no door in the far wall of the White Drawing Room, to connect it to the Closet where the Queen was waiting . . .

. . . She gave the signal exactly seventeen minutes before she was due to take her seat in the Ballroom.

Then, the Music Room was full, the tension highest, the sigh of polite amazement most satisfying when a section of the Drawing Room wall swung away, a tall mirror and a bookcase disappeared, and she stepped forward, into the brilliant world, the white and gold.

Forty-eight feet in front of her, the bodies of the guests shimmered and receded in the Music Room's pinky light. She advanced alone through stark magnificence, marking out her steps across the first of three enormous garlands down the middle of the carpet, passing flat columns with embellished gold edges, entangled with the gold life of mirror frames that twisted upwards on the white walls, giving the room its intoxicating verticality, the sense of everything shooting away into a light she could not yet face.

In the second ring of flowers, under the main chandelier, she lifted her head to accept the full radiance. One hundred and forty-four bulbs overhead, their light split and refracted down the tiers of pendulous fittings, and along the walls bronze figures held up ninety-six electric candles. Britannia thought the effect had never been so breathtaking. The surfaces of mirrors seemed multi-faceted, prismatic, sending up light at strange angles, to animate with shadows the sculpted cherubs of the frieze. But she could not be diverted, not be distracted now. She could not stop.

Society lapped at the double doors ahead. She was being propelled back into it, across the Drawing Room carpet. In the last few steps she felt a reassuring surge of congenital decorum. One could never entirely forget how to set one's face, staring straight ahead, slightly out of focus, thinking of nothing but the rhythmical fall of one's feet. She crossed the last floral circle without even wanting to look down, and left it behind as a wreath to her solitude.

Delicious just circulating, not talking, among the faces, voices, familiar and famous, of friends and members of the great family. Among the latter she finally, firmly placed that girl whom she had seen occasionally on the stairs and elsewhere. She was the ringleted Saxe-Coburg whose portrait hung downstairs in the Marble Hall. That military-looking man with her was her new husband, the Duke of Nemours, and he . . . Oh, it was so important not to forget these details about the people around one . . . Ah, she had it; he was the second son of the French King!

Ten minutes after her arrival among them, the first of the Queen's guests paired off for the long walk into dinner. Gracefully, imperceptibly, they all filtered away, and she was left alone in the Music Room, wishing for Tony again. But she had been brushed by the ineffable warm sweetness of the living, and this temporary desertion was just a prelude to her formal entrance, when she would take her place at the top of the horseshoe table. She lifted up her head and breathed deeply, waiting to walk. Tonight the dome of the Music Room seemed to be lined with stars.

The one-person Royal procession recommenced with the long Drawing Room of fraudulent onyx. Fifteen honey-veined columns along each wall were in fact cunningly painted plaster. Perhaps she was the only person now living who knew that. How many of her guests would believe that the Palace had deceived them?

The staff had been thorough in their preparations – she had never seen these windows so clean – and thoughtful: the carpet in this room was strewn with petals. And in the next, the scarlet State Dining Room, silvery gossamer hung in sheets from the ceiling.

On, to the West Gallery, which opened at its far end

into the Ballroom. She very nearly stopped to look at the superb Gobelins tapestries depicting scenes from Cervantes. Her favourite was the one in which the princess begged Don Quixote to restore her to her throne. That poignant, faded, mad-scene was still in Britannia's mind as she approached the last set of double doors.

For a moment, the great company of diners was spread before her, seated and at its ease, assured that in celebrating Her tonight, it celebrated the return of an England, a breadth, a standard, cherished through ages of meanness, enshrined in the real achievements of English culture.

Straight ahead, with his back to her, William Shakespeare was easily recognizable by his bald pate and straggling side-hair. On the far side of the horseshoe table was the equally unmistakable runt, Alexander Pope, who had arranged one of the early publications of *The Patriot King*. He was talking to Benjamin Disraeli. Dr Johnson sat nearby, occupying at least two chairs, looking around with a defensive scowl. Still looping his neck was the ribboned gold touch-piece he had received as a child from the hands of Queen Anne. There was Francis Drake, and John Nash, talking rapidly to Inigo Jones, no doubt complaining that this room they were in had *not* been included in his original design for the Palace. Blake was there, and Brunel, Turner, her Irish favourites Geldof and Wilde. And Elton John. Those last two seemed to have a great deal in common. Arthur Sullivan, on the other hand, would have nothing to do with Paul McCartney, and kept glancing up to the minstrel's gallery, as if waiting to hear his own music played. Britannia thought him silly; of course it would be played. Fortunately, Noël Coward and the Duke of Wellington were getting on splendidly. And Virginia

Woolf, who was hopping from conversation to conversation, dragging her chair from one end of the table to the other, looked as though she would burst with excitement, poor dear.

Then Britannia had arrived. The yeoman at the door signalled to the Musicians Gallery and the drums broke out, imposing silence on the guests, bringing them to their feet for *God Save the Queen*. She braced herself; this was a moment of the highest, most solemn emotion. But as she stepped into the Ballroom, there was a disturbance; the sound of someone moving in her wake with undignified haste, and an urgent voice, close behind, whispering, 'Your Majesty. Dreadful news!'

'Your Majesty!'

Having searched the North Wing, Edward arrived at the foot of the Ministers' Staircase, and shouted up. The stairwell was adequately moonlit, and there were footprints on the carpet, so he went as far as the Royal Closet, and stood in the space where the concealed door once hung.

'Your Majesty!'

He tried a light switch. Of course, the electricity to the West Front had been cut off, now that it was officially in disuse. He walked to the middle of the White Drawing Room, and looked around. This oldest part of the Palace had decayed most quickly; these walls were anything but white now, the big mirrors hung shattered in their frames, and the circumfluent frieze was animated by the scurrying shadows of rats.

The State Apartments stretched dimly away to the Ballroom. It would be too difficult to search them in the dark; he would call once more, then try the East Front. As he opened his mouth, he saw her. Instinctively, he raised his hand.

'Your Majesty.'

She was too far off, no bigger than his middle finger, and visible only intermittently as she passed through successive shafts of moonlight. He saw that she had dressed up in a wrecked Hartnell gown, and was walking slowly, trailing spangled chiffon, evidently engrossed by some fantasy. He walked forward without calling again.

The Music Room had lost its ceiling. Nash's much-imitated stucco dome had collapsed inwards with most of its outer cladding, exposing a starry circle of night sky. Edward crossed beneath it and into the pillared drawing room. Here the windows were out, removed whole by looters. The invading air had sucked flakes of white paint from the ceiling; it littered the carpet like petals.

She stopped in the West Gallery, giving him a chance to catch her up. He could have called to her from the State Dining Room, but in the light from the gallery's glass roof, it was clear that she had slipped into a state of extreme and dangerous distraction.

The condition was certainly classic. Christina would have a name for it; the mind's inability to accept certain outrages, certain losses. Could it reconstruct on blank walls the detail of those tapestries? Or obliterate from the memory that dreadful time, not so long ago, when the American collector had come to take them away?

He stood well back while she completed her ghostly appraisal, smiling to herself, the arms leading a queer autonomous life, fluttering around the folds of her dirty white rags, constantly arranging and adjusting, flying up to check her rhinestone tiara. It was frightening; he was sorry for her, sorry for everyone. But he was not defeated, and this mad old woman was still a useful weapon. He waited only until she started to move again, towards the lightless hole of the

Ballroom door, then rushed forward to shatter her reverie with a fresh deception.

She was furious, speechless. She stormed away, back through the State Apartments, down the Ministers' Staircase, Vane following at a respectful distance, confident of success. In the Garden Entrance Hall, she turned to him, all dreaminess replaced by a bright-eyed, serviceable madness.

'Mr Vane,' she said firmly. 'Will you wait in your office until I send for you? I must have a few minutes alone in my study, to decide what is to be done.'

He inclined his head in acquiescence, and escorted her to her lift. But as soon as she was out of sight, he hurried away down the Privy Purse Passage, not stopping at the door of his office. He already knew what was to be done.

He climbed the North-East Stairs and walked to the far end of the Chamber Corridor, to the sitting-room once occupied by Lady Bracken. He crossed to the window; the reliable crowd of tourists milled at the Palace railings, swapping postcards, waiting for something to happen. Ensuring that the curtains were open as far as possible, he returned to the door and switched on the light. No, it was too gloomy; that huge lotus chandelier would have to go. Propped in a corner was a prayer-wheel on a long wooden pivot. He picked it up to test its weight, then took it to the centre of the room and swung it at the chandelier. The green glass ruptured and spattered over him. He shut his eyes and struck again and again till the cluster of bulbs in the middle was completely exposed, and the room was as bright as it could be. Then he went into the next room along the corridor, taking the prayer-wheel with him, in case he should need it again to achieve the same effect.

The tourists were excited. Each new illumination was answered by a volley of bulb flashes from the street. The dull stone of the upper facade was now suffused with yellow light from twenty-three windows. And when the first chandeliers went on in the Principal Apartments, it became clear that something extraordinary, unremembered, was happening at the Palace tonight. The word went out, into the parks and up the Mall to Trafalgar Square. That was the Empire Suite that had been lit up, the Blue Rooms, the Yellow Rooms, the famous Centre Room with its balcony; yes, the Royal Balcony was lit now . . .

The word went out, and the numbers at the gate doubled. People came out of the trees and the underground. They arrived in taxis. Coaches were diverted to the Palace. The numbers trebled. And while they seethed and speculated outside, the phantom illuminating hand moved on to the Ground Floor.

Having worked his way back to the foot of the North-East stairs, he stopped and listened. The crowd was audible even from here, polite but ready to roar, satisfyingly roused. He went back to his office and drank three large whiskies to set himself up for the night's work. Then took the lift up to Britannia's study.

No light showed under the door. He entered abruptly, without rattling the handle, braced for some last-minute disaster.

But she was sitting in her chair in the bay window; moonlit, asleep. Her tiara was on the carpet at her feet. He stood in front of her, allowing room for the desk, and cleared his throat. She did not wake up. He picked up the tiara and moved behind her to place it on the tangled white hair. 'Your Majesty.' He shook her gently by the shoulders and she gave a little squeak. 'Your Majesty.' He bent down and spoke softly into her ear. 'The People are waiting.'

What if they were horrified by her decrepitude? She remembered the image presented by the Patriot Party leaflet; herself years younger, dark-haired, preternaturally healthy.

But when the Balcony doors were opened, and the crowd began to chant her name, she could not believe they would reject her. The call was irresistible, doubt-cancelling. Standing under the lights in the Centre Room she knew she could only move forward. The birds in the wallpaper knew it too, and hopped frantically about in the fruit trees, impatient for her to go, not to miss the chance, to break out of the old decorative pattern, and live.

'Breetaania! Breetaania! Breetaania!'

Vane jostled through the crowd, wearing a solar topee, waving a plastic Union Jack on a stick, and bawling for the Queen. His commitment fired Continental enthusiasm. They saw his wild eyes, laughed, reached out to touch his hat, and shouted all the louder, 'Breetaania! Breetaania!'

When she appeared, he was able to rest at the back. The hysteria vented itself without further encouragement. Certainly she made a compelling spectacle; small and self-contained under her rhinestone crown, with the Palace blazing behind. Perhaps the very strangeness of her appearance certified her authenticity. At any rate the tourists went crazy for her, their greeting settled at a reverberating climax which lasted for two full minutes until she raised her right hand and suddenly achieved silence. It was a consummate gesture. Her authority reached to the edges of the crowd. Edward gasped. 'My God. The woman's a natural!'

She began to speak in her once-familiar, high-pitched voice. After years without practice, her delivery was erratic, but the tourists strained to hear her, and seized on every word that reached them. 'Patriot Paarty!' a tall Swede near Edward exclaimed delightedly, and squeezed his girlfriend's hand. She smiled up at him and giggled, 'Patriot Paarty!'

'Electoral coruuption.' 'Intolerable eensult.' 'Eenglish deegnity.' Everywhere they were picking up words and phrases, repeating them, passing them on; intrigued, amused, but entirely uncomprehending. It was a pity really; even from his position at the back, Edward could tell that the speech was magnificent. But the English syllables tumbling from the Balcony were as mysterious to her audience as the woman who spoke them.

As she warmed up, releasing her indignation, Britannia started to infuse her words with a certain fibrous durability, and if Edward made an effort he could hear them at first hand.

'My People,' she was saying, 'it comes to this: I am asking you to help me restore this Kingdom. I am offering you a revitalized Monarchy, a new pride for Britain, and you must give your answer. Your electoral system can no longer be trusted; it appears that Democracy will protect itself by any undemocratic means. You must find another way to make your feelings known. Before you can offer me your loyalty, you must let our present leaders know that they no longer have it. Before you come to seal this contract with me, you must take our case to Downing Street!'

She stopped, waved briefly, then left the Balcony. The tourists waited in silence for something else to happen. They looked at one another, they looked at the empty Balcony. Then someone at the back began to shout, 'To Downing Street! To Downing Street!'

People at the front turned round and recognized the bobbing white hat, the waving plastic flag. What was he saying? Somebody near him took up the call, 'To Dow Ning Street!' And it spread through the crowd: 'To Dow Ning Street!'

They forgot about the Palace. Everyone was straining for a glimpse of the white hat, trying out the new words: 'To Dow Ning Street.' 'Todown Ing Street.'

The man in the white hat capered in front of them. Was he a busker? Some said he was the Queen's personal clown, sent to entertain them. Now he wanted them to follow him somewhere. He was a tour guide then. Who cared? He was fun, he was photogenic, he was an English eccentric!

So they went along; a foreign legion in tracksuits and airline slippers, laughing and shouting, up the Mall, 'Todown Ingstreet!'

14

In the Prime Minister's sitting-room, they were celebrating with a game of Monopoly. Tadpole was doing well, but the Home Secretary and the Chancellor were at each others' throats. Garbo was present, but did not play. He stood with his drink, in front of the fire, watching the game. What did it matter if they never knew that he had saved them? Washington knew. Washington was pleased.

He looked at his watch. Late. And he liked to have the evenings to himself. Soon, a fierce dispute broke out over Bond Street and while the players glared and bickered, he left the room.

From the hallway, he could hear some sort of disturbance in the street. He started to walk towards the front of the house, but a stranger appeared suddenly from one of the rooms, and stood in his way, hand outstretched.

'Major Garbo?' he said, 'We haven't met. Edward Vane, Secretary to the Secretary.'

Garbo did not accept the hand. 'Aren't you the guy who tried to blackmail the Government?'

'The same.' Edward grinned. 'Quarter of a million

pounds. That's why I'm here now as a matter of fact, to collect it.'

Garbo chuckled and shook his head. 'You're welcome to try my friend. Right now, Tadpole is having a nervous breakdown over half that amount of toy money!'

'I realize it might be difficult,' said Vane. 'Particularly as my party lost the election anyway. That's why I'd like you to help me . . . to soften them up . . . Perhaps you could tell them how you fixed the result.'

Garbo said nothing. He brought his eyebrows together in a vee; astonished-innocence-acting. Vane walked away to the end of the hall, and opened a window. He stuck out his head, and a great shout greeted him. 'Todown Ingstreet! Todown Ingstreet! He withdrew from the window and closed it behind him. The chanting outside continued.

'There must be a thousand of them now,' said Vane. 'More arriving all the time.'

'What are they saying?' Garbo asked.

'You have to understand that the English people don't take kindly to electoral corruption. Whatever it is they're chanting now, you can be certain that pretty soon they'll be calling for your blood.'

'Don't bullshit me, Vane!' Garbo marched up and peeped out at the crowd. 'This stuff about the election is crap, and you know it!'

'Even if it were, you'd still swear to the truth of it.' Edward was sweetly smiling.

Garbo stared, but no explanation followed. He went on acting. 'This crowd is a threat to the Prime Minister's security. I'm going to have it cleared. Your English police are good at that.'

He walked away down the hall, but Edward called after him.

'And the English press are good at exposing . . . what's the American word? Faggots?'

Garbo didn't turn round. 'What the hell are you talking about?'

Edward called, 'Damon.'

Damon came out of the room from which Vane had appeared, and stood a few feet away from Garbo. A second later Peter Pounce also entered the hall.

'Show him, Damon,' said Vane. And Damon dropped his jeans to show the red initials. Vane sidled up behind the American. 'I'd call that a signed confession, Major.'

The noise from the street having at last disturbed the Monopoly game, Tadpole came out of his sitting-room to discover a boy in the hall with his trousers round his ankles.

'Major Garbo,' he asked, 'are these people friends of yours?'

'Tell him now,' said Vane.

Garbo took a deep breath. 'I have to advise you Alex, that the by-election is void . . . I fixed the result.'

Tadpole winced. He took off his glasses and rubbed his eyes. 'But I told you it wasn't necessary,' he said wearily. 'No one is interested in this . . . Patriot Party.

'Well THEY seem to be!' Garbo gestured towards the demonstrators.

Tadpole replaced his glasses and went to the window. 'They look like tourists to me.' He listened for a moment. 'Does anyone know what they're saying?'

'Mr Tadpole.' Edward came forward. The Prime Minister looked alarmed.

'Who on earth are you?'

'Vane, sir, Sec to the Sec.'

'Ah! You're the one who . . .'

'Yes sir, the money. Quarter of a million. I'm here to collect it.'

'Collect!' Tadpole's moustache shot up to his nose.

He made a comic mental effort, his lower lip thrust out fish-like, striving at the air. Damon giggled. Then the Prime Minister began to sway on his feet, and Garbo came forward.

'Look, Alex, I really think . . . all things considered . . .' He couldn't keep his eyes off the window. Outside the mob howled incomprehensible demands. Vane stood back, happy to wait.

'Alex.' Garbo spoke firmly, holding Tadpole's shoulders, holding his frightened stare. 'Washington would prefer it.'

Nothing more to be said. Nothing to be explained when Washington spoke. Tadpole recovered quickly, and bowed slightly to Vane.

'I'll have the Chancellor make out a cheque immediately . . . to you I suppose.'

'No,' Edward said slowly. 'It's too late. I can't use it now. Have it made out to Her Majesty The Queen.'

He went with Tadpole into the sitting-room, leaving Pounce and his enemy alone together. Pounce contemplated the disgraced handsome boots.

'I'll get you for this, bastard.' Garbo was calm and clear. 'Think of me when you're lying in bed.' Pounce looked up quickly and bared his teeth, then followed the others without speaking. Words could not spoil or sweeten the fact of his victory.

Damon also started towards the sitting-room. But the American got in his way and put a hand on his shoulder. 'How are you son?' He smiled. 'You're looking a lot better.' Damon made no effort to move away. 'I've got the bike outside,' Garbo went on. 'How about coming for a burn?'

Damon looked up, smiled back, and kicked him in the balls.

Vane came out a few minutes later, clutching his cheque, and found Garbo sitting on a chair in the hall.

'Ah Major, I'm glad you're still here. There's something else you can do for me. Keep your trucks out of the Mall on Sundays. You can find an alternative route can't you, if you try?'

Garbo nodded, unable to speak.

She could not bear to withdraw completely from that supportive popular presence. After leaving the Balcony, Britannia remained in the Centre Room, to hear the cry go up, the sound of men making history, to feel herself in a sense carried before them, as they marched up the Mall to Downing Street. From a comfortable chair by the open door she listened to the chorus diminishing, diminishing, then rising again, reassuring, on a wave, just as her thoughts were beginning to sink . . .

She got up groggily from her chair, aware that she had slept. There was no sound outside now, only the familiar murmurings of the Palace. She went into the Principal Corridor and started to walk towards the North-East Stairs. The Corridor was dark, but from every door wide bands of light cut across it. By means of one of these, she saw that someone was coming toward her. At first it was a long way off: the figure of a tall woman, which passed again into darkness so quickly that Britannia almost doubted its existence. But then it was suddenly much closer, in another band of light, more real than ever, yet more spectral, moving mechanically, bearing on outstretched arms some sort of ghastly, shrouded cargo.

Britannia matched the speed of the approaching apparition. A sense of personal destiny, banishing fear, propelled her toward the strip of light in which they would meet. As she arrived, the woman entered from the opposite side. Britannia saw a wasted, but unmistakably German face. She struggled to identify it, to fix it in the family, find the Blood connection.

Yet the woman hardly glanced at her, did not recognize relative or ruler. The deep-set eyes swivelled from Britannia's face to the room in whose light they were standing. 'Is that the room of Edward Vane?' she asked.

Britannia was taken aback. 'No,' she said, 'he lives on the next floor up.'

It was a boy the woman carried; once almost a man, to judge by the length of him, but now emaciated, bone-light. His face peeped out from the swaddling blanket, expressionless, infinitely tired. Britannia could tell that he had only a few hours to live.

Nothing could make Edward happy, or ease the sense of failure. But after a turbulent day, he had salvaged something from the Patriot Party, and he came home along the Chamber Corridor humming to himself, his fingers on the cheque in his pocket. At the door of his room he stopped singing, stopped and stared at a tableau there: Britannia standing by his bed, her gown incandescent with light from the yellow walls, the costume tiara still on her head. And next to her, Erika, kneeling, bent slightly forward to watch her son's face.

As he came further into the room, Erika turned, and stood up to meet him. He saw Ian's face, but hardly recognized it. The flesh had already taken on an unfamiliar colour and texture; only a bird-breathing, the slightest rise and fall of the bedclothes, indicated life. Edward was disgusted, afraid, but sustained by a sense of gratitude; she wanted to share this worst moment with him. He started to speak, but she cut him short.

'I suppose you thought it was over already!' He was startled by the indecorous tone. He needed to pull her away from the bed, to calm her down.

'Erika, please, forgive me for not coming. I felt so useless.' He took her arm, but she wrenched it free.

'Don't you touch me! What right do you have to touch me? What right did you ever have?'

He gaped at her. If he were to mention love, she would spit at him, he was certain of it. There was no vein of sympathy in her to tap. She hated him. She had brought Ian here only in order to punish him. He was useless to her, loathsome. He realized that everything she had given him, everything promised, had been mere good will, credit, advance payment for saving Ian's life.

The boy, asleep now, and the old woman standing over him were equally unaware of the embittered lovers. Britannia was at the head of the bed; the tableau had reformed in Erika's absence, closing her out. Could she see the perfection of the new arrangement? Did she understand that it must be preserved? In case not, Edward took her arm again when she started to walk away from him. She rounded, angry, but her rebuke was cancelled this time, by the expression on his face, the tightness of his grip, holding her, turning her back to witness a single, undramatic gesture. An arm extended, a touch on damp skin, something that passed from the standing to the supine body, from the Queen to her subject, and Ian opened his eyes.

'Mr Vane?' Britannia continued to look down, to meet Ian's first enquiring look, 'Do you have a pound coin?'

He felt in his pockets, then remembered having to borrow earlier, to make a phone call.

'I have one, I think,' said Erika, not understanding.

'Give it to the Queen,' Edward whispered, and let her go.

He stayed long enough to watch Britannia hold out the coin to Ian, who reached up and took it firmly in his hand.

15

'Couldn't it be fixed?'

'Probably.' Christina dropped her shoe into Edward's wastepaper basket, 'But I'm sick of them. Bloody sick. Where's that coffee? I've broken up with Fox-Peeper, by the way; absolutely.'

'Oh? Why?'

'I can't make myself love him enough to imagine he has a big cock.'

'At least your men know from the start what you want them for.'

'Oh Teddy, don't mope. I rely on you to cheer me up in the mornings.'

'Sorry. Where did you break your heel anyway?'

'One of those fissures in the North-East Stairs. I hope she uses that money to have some repairs done around here.'

'She won't need to. Tadpole's authorized a complete renovation, and re-staffing. He'll be good for these little favours so long as Garbo's on our side. Which reminds me, I must get Pounce to photograph the evidence.'

'Superficial injuries heal quickly at that age.'

'Yes, better get it while it's nice and scabby. I'll ring him this morning.' He made a note on his desk jotter. Christina walked over to look out of the window.

'It wasn't just his cock though . . . I'm beginning to think that I might have, well, standards. You know, festering, deep down, something you can't ever properly grow out of, like looking forward to Christmas.'

He laughed at her, but she would not face him.

'It's just that I don't want to be living like this when I'm forty. Treating people like shit, and believing that they deserve it.'

'Some of them aren't too bad.'

'No . . . What about Albert Bridge? Did you ever find out how he got on in Islington?'

'Oh yes. McShane told me just before he topped himself . . . to make his venality seem less crucial.'

'Ah. Albert had lost in any case.'

'Handsomely. But he hasn't done too badly out of it. Britannia tried some of his bread, and liked it. She's appointed him Baker to the new Household. D'you fancy lunch at John Wayne's?'

'That might be nice . . .' She turned and smiled at him. 'And perhaps a little Blue Bedroom afterwards? It's almost warm today.'

'I can't offer you cocaine you know.'

She shrugged, walking slowly to his desk. 'I'd still like to know if Britannia does have any popular support. How many votes did the Patriot Party get, exactly?'

He looked up at her and shook his head.

'*None*?'

'None,' he affirmed.

16

Damon woke up hot, breathless. In the next bed Watcher snored quietly. From further off came the sound of Microbe's fretful snuffling. Damon had been frightened by a dream. He threw off his top blanket and lay back, playing with his cock to soothe himself. He let it swell, then took his hand away; too messy to go on. He turned on his side to sleep. And when he began to doze a voice, very close, said: 'Slimy! Squash it!'

Watcher was talking in his sleep. His carroty head was thrashing around on his pillow. Damon got up and put on jeans and a shirt. He took one of Watcher's cigarettes as compensation and wandered out to smoke it in the Common Room.

The lights had been switched off, but there was still a good fire. He sat hunched forward in one of the armchairs, smoking nervously, drumming with his bare feet on the floor, watching the flames jump.

Suddenly, he flopped back in the chair and gazed up at the dome. Tonight its roughness was shaded over, its capacity seemed huge, a hemisphere in darkness, with scudding clouds of firelight. Those orangey clouds made it a city sky. His sky.

'It'll have to come down I'm afraid.'

Damon let out his pent-up breath. The prematurely wizened face of Peter Pounce had come between him and the dome. 'Why?' he said, not sitting up.

'It's no longer safe. Those support beams are rotting.'

Damon looked past him at the crude wooden framework. 'Don't need 'em anyway. There's this new stuff, I read about it. It's called Plasteel. It's light and strong, and dead easy to install. We could . . .'

He saw that Peter was nodding at what he said, but the smile on his face was sort of dreamy. And his eyes, they had that look that some men got when they're standing over you, and you're sprawled out in a chair, not caring . . .

What was it about this Pounce, this soft-looking queer schoolteacher? What made you want to keep in his good books, when you'd never given a fuck what adults thought? It wasn't the food and shelter; you could get them at home. Of course, he was more understanding than anyone at home. But then, queers are always understanding.

Peter crossed in front of him to poke at the fire. It was nothing you could see, nothing you could envy, like the Yank with the muscles and the boots and the bike.

'You did well at Downing Street the other day . . . Peter was saying. Yes, he was a good worker now, one of the Brewery Boys, but not quite. '. . . Which reminds me, I had a call from Edward Vane. He wants me to get some photos of those initials before they heal . . .' Funny, how the thing he was most curious about was the one thing never openly discussed by the boys. '. . . We could do it now, in fact. I've got a camera in my room . . .' What was it like, sleeping with Peter Pounce? He had always known that sooner or later, he would have to find out for himself.

So far, nothing much had happened. Peter was like one of those men who come up to you at a bus stop and invite you home to watch a video or have a few beers. They always had their sly routine, giving you a chance to call it off at every stage, and pretend nothing had happened, before pressing on towards the big thrill: a grope and a quick wank. Most queers seemed to enjoy the seduction more than the sex. The American had been different of course; just thinking about it made him bite the pillow.

He had stripped off his jeans and stretched out, face down on the bed in the alcove, so that Peter could take pictures of his arse. Afterwards, Peter had offered to check the wounds for signs of infection, and his fingers had made contact. 'Does that hurt?' he had asked, and he moved his hand away . . . to rest it absent-mindedly on the back of Damon's thigh while they talked.

All the time, Damon had been answering questions about his past life. Now they were on to his experiences with girls. Peter knew a surprising amount, and Damon was encouraged to tell everything that had happened to him. Then he went on to speculate about things that hadn't. This imagining had brought on the hard pressure between his body and the bed.

Had Peter opened a window? With nothing but a shirt on, Damon was getting cold. Peter commented that his skin was covered in goose bumps, running his hand playfully to the back of Damon's knee. And said that he would be warmer under the blankets . . .

So here he was, sitting up in bed, watching Peter Pounce undress. The body was thin and hairy, and when a white card fell out of a shirt pocket, Damon reached out and picked it up, glad of something else to look at. It was a calling card, similar to the one Peter had given him when they first met. He remembered those two difficult words. 'Anguis,' he read aloud. 'Bi . . . cep . . .'

'Bicephalous.' Pounce unbuckled his belt.

'Why d'you have those big words anyway?'

'Impresses boys when I meet them in the street. It impressed you.' He smiled down at Damon and took off his trousers. 'Of course even big words have meanings.'

Damon put the card aside and stretched out with his hands clasped behind his head. He smiled back. 'Well, what does this Anguis Bi . . . cephalous mean then?'

Pounce slipped off his briefs. 'Two-headed snake.'

'Fuckin' Jesus! What the hell is *that*?' Damon wriggled away across the bed, taking the blankets for protection, and bunched himself up against the window, looking for an escape. There was cold glass behind him and a forty-foot drop outside, on every side, into the canal. He squirmed. He whimpered. He made threats, made himself ugly. But in the end there was nothing to do except face the front, that advancing antlerian appendage, and the watery eyes of the schoolteacher, offering no quarter.

Peter Pounce sat up in bed. What was it? Had Damon kicked him in his sleep? He looked down at the exhausted boy. No, it was a sound that had woken him, rather than a physical shock; something that had been nagging at his sleep for hours. The noises of a threatening dream. He would remember its detail tomorrow. At the moment there was quiet, and grey light along the canal, hurrying him back to finish his sleep before morning.

Now there were pictures: the floor beneath his bed; it was a trapdoor in fact. He saw the huge bolt that held it in place, and mysterious hands at work. They were loosening the bolt, but it was stiff. Flakes of rust fell away to the freezing water. He watched, fascinated, as the strong hands eased it, centimetre by centimetre, towards release. Whose hands were they, he wondered. Why would anybody go to such trouble? . . .

He lunged across and took hold of Damon's inert body, rolling it back, pulling him out of the alcove, panting to get off the bed in time. Then the world split open. Pounce screamed as the cold air hit him and the bed flipped out into space. His hands were locked to the sides of the mattress, but Damon's still unconscious body slid away on its own. Pounce saw him for a second, suspended, his white flesh floating, the back sculpturally arched, arms and legs flung out, starlike.

Corporal Fletcher had laughed and punched the air in triumph when Pounce splashed down. Something going on there, Garbo thought. He stood on the opposite bank, watching Fletcher swing away from the ruptured alcove, hand over hand on his line across the water. He had been sullen all along, always the same when English soldiers were seconded to American command. Garbo had personally picked him from the SAS; efficiency was the only consideration. But then, right at the end, that show of personal malice, the big grin that was still on his face as he landed on the Waitings side.

'I told him that thing wasn't safe,' he said, starting to pack his equipment. 'There was a lot still needed doing.'

Garbo walked away without speaking. The English army was full of misfits. Further down the canal he passed Pounce's bed, bumping against the pillar of a bridge.

17

Another summer; one too many. Michael Felter's eyes were half closed against the light. There was too much of it, too much heat. His deckchair was set at the reclining position, and he waited listlessly, feeling slightly sick, for the sun to move behind the plane trees, move him into shadow.

Although he no longer enjoyed the park, he came every Sunday, to police the exclusion of traffic from the Mall. Although he would be dead soon, and was not sorry to think of it, people would continue to enjoy this quiet day, preserved for them because a socialist had written an angry letter.

> But somewhere some word presses
> On the high door of a skull, and in some corner
> Of an irrefrangible eye
> Some old man's memory jumps to a child
> —Spark from the days of energy.
> And the child hoards it like a bitter toy.

Spender's poem had concluded with that hope for Spain. But who would learn from Felter's example? What promising English bitterness had not been stifled now by pessimism and the meanness of beleaguered lives?

In front of him, a grim-looking, fair-haired woman helped a sickly youth across the lawn. The nuclear family. That boy had no energy to spare for political ideals, and the woman lived only to nurse him.

THE GLAMOUR

CHRISTOPHER PRIEST

All Richard Grey wanted to do was recover, to return to normal. For four long, painful months he had been convalescing after the horrifying injuries that he sustained when a car bomb exploded near him.

He could remember the years he spent as a cameraman, covering stories all over the world, and he could remember taking a break from his career – but there was a profound blankness where his memory of the weeks before the explosion should have been. It was as if his life had been re-edited and part of it erased.

But then Susan Kewley came to visit him and she spoke of those weeks. And what Richard wanted most was a glimpse of what that time had held for the two of them. But the glimpses he was afforded took him into a strange and terrible twilight world – a world of apparent madness, the world of 'the glamour' . . .

Christopher Priest's rich and subtle narrative is mesmerising and deeply moving, as compelling and deceptive as a Hitchcock film.

'One of our most gifted writers.' *John Fowles*

'A bizarre and intriguing book.' *Guardian*

ABACUS FICTION 0 349 128103 £2.95

OUT NOW IN PAPERBACK:

WINNER OF THE PULITZER PRIZE FOR FICTION

"Brightly lit, fluently shaped, the story is a ballet that dances rings round the English way of life"

MAIL ON SUNDAY

"There is no American writer I have read with more constant pleasure and sympathy over the years. FOREIGN AFFAIRS earns the same shelf as Henry James and Edith Wharton"

JOHN FOWLES

"Alison Lurie is not only the most elegant novelist in America today – she is also one of the strongest"

OBSERVER

"A brilliant novel – her best . . . witty, acerbic and sometimes fiendishly clever . . . a triumph"

PAUL BAILY THE STANDARD

"FOREIGN AFFAIRS is warm, clever and funny"

THE TIMES LITERARY SUPPLEMENT

"Alison Lurie is a writer of extraordinary talent . . . she is perhaps more shocking than she knows – shocking like Jane Austen, not Genet"

CHRISTOPHER ISHERWOOD

FICTION 0 349 122156 £3.50

ALSO BY ALISON LURIE IN ABACUS:

LOVE AND FRIENDSHIP
THE WAR BETWEEN THE TATES
THE NOWHERE CITY

"If you've never bought a book about rock and roll, no matter – this is the one you've been waiting for." PLAYBOY

The True Adventures of THE ROLLING STONES

Stanley Booth

IT LEAVES NO STONE UNTURNED:

"Stanley Booth gets closer to the essence of the Rolling Stones and their world than any previous author. It is the only book about the Stones I would recommend both to the general reader and to the most devoted fan."
Robert Palmer NEW YORK TIMES

"Easily the best study of Mick, Keith and Co." TIME OUT

0 349 103577 ABACUS NON-FICTION £3.95

His most ambitious novel to date . . .

ANTHONY BURGESS

THE KINGDOM OF THE WICKED

This is an extraordinary account of the first years of Christianity, recreated in vivid and meticulous detail.

"Burgess takes hold of an immense theme with magnificent mastery. Detail and dialogue are incredibly vivid; one hardly knows which to praise most".

LITERARY REVIEW

"All Burgess's skills are in evidence here: his ornate imagination, his fascination with words, his sly wit, the prodigious energy . . ."

LONDON STANDARD

"His unassuageable energy can do nothing other than celebrate the energy of life itself".

SUNDAY TIMES

"Both reader and author have marvellous fun".

SUNDAY TELEGRAPH

0 349 10439 5 ABACUS FICTION £3.95

Also by Anthony Burgess in Abacus:

ENDERBY'S DARK LADY

he debut of an enormously gifted writer

Ease

■ PATRICK GALE ■

Domina Tey is one of life's success stories: an award-winning playwright, living with an equally celebrated writer in a magazine-featured home. A lucky woman, who knows and appreciates it. But at the moment, she's just not happy.

Convinced that a spell of seedy living – so far denied her by fate and circumstance – would give both work and soul a much-needed spring-clean, she elopes with her typewriter in search of la sleazy vita – discovering it in Bayswater's tarnished bedsit jungle. Within a week she has settled into the warm friendly world of Lady Tilly (landlady and ex-mortician), all-night sauna 'clubs' and midnight snack-land; and her search for a fresh start becomes an overwhelming desire to make passionate love to a much younger man. Quintus disturbs her. He's too innocent for such suffering. Domina watches his guilt changing shape, volume, direction, transforming him. Observing her, he carefully eases her out of her distress.

ABACUS FICTION 0 349 11400 5 £3.50

Patrick Gale's THE AERODYNAMICS OF PORK is also available in Abacus.